One Day in a Lifetime

Dave Heaver

ISBN 978-1-78792-001-9

Book design, layout and production management by Into Print
www.intoprint.net
+44 (0)1604 832149

Introduction

Welcome to my collection of short-stories which I have written over several years. Some are based around actual historic events which have held a fascination for me over the years. Some were inspired by actual personal experiences in my lifetime, others are simply the product of my imagination.

There is 'micro fiction', some 'short-short' stories and others which are longer, but what most of them demonstrate is how anyone's life can change, unplanned, for better or worse, in an instant. Fate, kismet, chance or destiny, whatever you call it, none of us knows what tomorrow will bring or what surprises are in store.

Dedication

To Sara, for her love, friendship and support, and for giving me the confidence and self-belief which has turned my dream into reality.

Contents

The Winning Ticket

"Do you remember the old man who used to live across the road?" Dad asked, briefly lifting his eyes from the local *Hampshire Chronicle* newspaper.

"Which one?" Mum replied without pausing from her ironing.

"You know, old Wilson, the bloke who had that Triumph motorbike?"

"Oh yes, I remember him."

"Well, he won that competition for two tickets on the cruise to New York, lucky devil. How come that kind of luck never happens to us?"

I looked up from my book, "You'll get your cruise next week Dad, even if it will be a working journey, at least it's a brand-new ship," I offered, in an attempt to cheer him up. "And not everyone gets to go on a maiden voyage do they? That will be something to remember in the future."

He sat there in his armchair, the newspaper flopping in his hands. His head leaned back on the white antimacassar and he closed his eyes as his mind drifted through the ship. Up from the starkly efficient engine rooms with the huge reciprocating engines, turbines and massive, riveted boilers – the heart of the ship Dad called them; through the

1

comfortable, panelled lower decks and up the magnificent solid oak Grand Staircase into the lavishly decorated upper levels with their sumptuous first-class staterooms.

"Not quite the same as being up there with the toffs though is it? That Wilson is one lucky bugger," he muttered, and turned his eyes back to his newspaper. His mind however took him, his cut-crystal Cognac glass and his Cuban cigar into the first-class smoking room where the carved mahogany panels were inlaid with mother of pearl, and on to the small veranda area with its walled trellises, wicker chairs and climbing plants. If only he'd won …

The following Tuesday afternoon Dad was getting ready to join the ship. Mum was fussing as usual before he went. "I'm only going for a couple of weeks Joyce," he complained good-naturedly as she packed his old, battered kit bag.

"I know," she smiled, "But I'm not having you running out of anything while you're away and spending all your, or should I say *our* money in New York Frederick Hawkins."

He put his arm around her shoulder and hugged her. "You're one in a million love; thanks."

A sharp knock at the door broke the tender moment. It was Jack, Dad's workmate of many years. Removing his cap as he came in he nodded towards Mum. "Afternoon Joyce, Dolly says to pop round for a cuppa sometime while we're away," before turning to Dad. "Come on 'awkins, the lads are all going for a quick pint before we join the ship, and you're invited," he grinned. "Put the missus down, grab your kit and let's go."

Dad gave Mum a kiss and ruffled my hair as he picked up his kit bag and followed Jack out of the door. He turned and smiled as he closed the door, "See you," and he was gone …

The following afternoon, Mum and I stood along with hundreds of others on the dockside, dwarfed by the magnificent vessel as just after midday she slipped her mooring lines and away into the narrow channel that leads to the open sea. The band was playing on deck and the ship's rails were lined with passengers, everyone cheering and waving with great excitement. But there was not much point in us waving; Dad would be far below deck by now, no doubt sweating furiously in the depths of the engine room. Maiden voyages just don't happen every day and I'd been allowed to skip school to watch the huge liner leave. I'd never seen such a magnificent ship.

This was quite a day and in addition to the general excitement surrounding the departure, there was a further moment of drama. As she passed close to another vessel, the *SS New York*, which was moored in the channel, there was almost a disaster. Suction from the big liner's wake caused the *New York* to break all of her mooring ropes and her stern swung out alarmingly to within about four feet of the big liner. It took nearly an hour to safely manoeuvre the pair but finally the *New York* was towed to a different mooring post and the tugs steered the new White Star liner away from danger. It was such an exciting day and I was so happy that I was there to see it all.

"Come on Billy," said Mum, "let's go home and get some tea."

"Alright; bye Dad," I muttered as I turned one final time and watched as the elegantly sculptured stern of the *RMS Titanic* steamed slowly away, "See you soon," and we set off for home.

Around five o'clock, half way through my tea, the front door suddenly flew open with a bang and a figure stumbled in. "Bugger! Now I'm in trouble."… It was Dad, looking very sheepish, unshaven and definitely the worse for wear.

"What in God's name are you doing here Fred?" Mum demanded, hands planted firmly on hips.

"I … I mean we … um, well," he stammered.

"We what? Come on, out with it man. Why aren't you on your way to New York?"

"Well, we must have had a couple too many in the pub last night and as Dolly was at her sister's, I stayed over at Jack's place instead of getting on the ship. I s'pose it must have been more than a couple because we didn't wake up until 10 o'clock. We ran down to join her but we were too late. We tried to get onboard but when we hadn't turned in last night they'd hired replacements and just told us to get lost; so we just went and had a few more drinks. I'm sorry love … really." He wobbled unsteadily and grabbed the edge of the table for support.

"Sorry? You're a bloody disgrace Fred Hawkins. What on earth were you thinking? That would have been a nice secure, long-term job on a brand-new ship like that. What are we going to live on now? Go and clean yourself up, I'll talk to you later," and with that, Dad headed dejectedly towards the stairs.

He paused as he passed me and smiled weakly. "If only I'd won that competition son … How come that kind of luck never happens to us?"

***

Cherchez la Femme

Jennifer's mind was blank as she stared out of the side window of her father's silver Volvo. She saw everything but registered nothing.

"Are you OK love?" her mother asked gently from the front passenger seat, "You're very quiet."

Jenny smiled. She knew her mum was just being kind but she really didn't want to talk about it.

"I'm fine Mum, really."

Her mother turned and winked at her, "Don't worry love, everything happens for a reason, even this," and she turned back to watch the road ahead.

Jenny knew she was right – it just didn't seem like it just now – her first Christmas without Tony after seven years together. Tears began to well in her eyes as she pushed blonde hair off her face and resumed her gaze out of the window, absurdly noticing the first event that had registered with her on the journey. In a small parking area just off the shingle beach, a middle-aged man emerged from a grey concrete toilet block and jumped directly into the passenger seat of a white pick-up truck that was parked immediately outside the door as if it were a limousine. *Now that's what you call service* she thought, smiling to herself. What a thing to notice, but it had made her smile for the first time in a long while.

"That's better; drive on Michael," commanded a relieved Jack as he climbed into the high cab of the Toyota. "Must be the coffee and the cold weather playing tricks on my internals."

"Hmm, so nothing to do with all that wine last night then?" grinned Mike as he swung the truck through 180 degrees and headed back to the road.

"Course not, I only had one bottle."

"And half of my red."

"Oh yeah. No, I'm sure it's the coffee. Anyway, what were we talking about before the pit stop?"

"Why we never seem to have any luck with women if my memory serves me right" grumbled Mike, "There must be somebody out there who would appreciate a couple of old farts like us."

"Of course there is. Trust me Michael, next year is going to be our year."

"Didn't we say that last year?" said Mike, absently scratching his bald patch.

"And probably the year before too," smiled Jack. "But this year I have a feeling in my water."

"Which you have just carelessly left behind in that concrete khazi by the roadside."

"Cynic!"

The big diesel engine clattered noisily under the bonnet

as the Toyota swung left and picked up speed and the two friends headed towards the cobbled streets of the picturesque ancient seaside town.

"I really don't want to talk about it Mum," Jenny protested as they parked the Volvo and walked towards the town but as with so many caring mothers, Ellen was not so easily dissuaded.

"But did he say why?" she persisted, "He always seemed so ... well, sensible."

"Mum!"

"Ellie, for goodness sake leave the poor girl alone." The voice of Jenny's usually quiet father, Ted. "She's thirty-one years old and she just wants a peaceful day out ... as do I," he scolded jovially. He draped his arm around Ellen's shoulders and winked at Jenny who, for the first time, noticed the old-fashioned habit shared by both her parents. "Now who's for coffee and cake, on me?" he offered.

Wife and daughter both started to laugh, "He knows just how to get around us every time," said Ellen.

"Thanks Daddy, that would be lovely," added Jenny hugging his arm.

They paused at the pedestrian crossing as a Harley Davidson motorcycle thumped past noisily, then they crossed the road and headed up into the old town as a white pick-up truck appeared around the sea wall to their right.

"It must be twenty years since I've been here," said Jack

as they tried unsuccessfully to find a space in the Pay and Display closest to the town, "and you couldn't park here back then either if I remember rightly."

"You should see it in the summer," Mike remarked, swinging the truck out of the car park and back to the road. "Left or right?"

"Right, away from the town," Jack answered, "you know how people hate to walk too far. We'll have more luck away from the centre. Anyway, after that Chinese last night, the walk will do us good," he added, patting his stomach.

"Yeah, bad enough being a couple of old farts without being fat old farts," Mike grinned.

Five minutes later the truck was parked and Mike and Jack were looking at the sadly neglected boats in the harbour.

"Must be nice to have thirty grand's-worth of boat sitting here rotting away," commented Jack, noticing the green growth on the furled sails of one particular small yacht that didn't look as though it had troubled the sea for a very long time.

"This one looks more used," said Mike as they passed a larger but still tatty cabin cruiser. "It has a kettle in there and some new wood around the windows."

Jack surveyed the sad little craft with its peeling paint and wooden deck devoid of varnish. "Looks more like somebody's maritime garden shed to me. He probably comes down here to get away from the wife," he joked as they walked on towards the town.

Both having been motorcyclists in their younger days, they paused for a moment to look at half a dozen bikes parked in an area opposite the boats.

I thought I heard a Harley," commented Jack, noticing a black and maroon Dyna Glide as its rider, a man in his mid-fifties, sat on the wall alongside, smoking a roll-up.

"I'd prefer the Ninja," replied Mike, pointing to the lime-green Kawasaki a few yards away.

"Nah, I'm getting too old for those *rip-yer-arms-off* sportsbikes. Been there, done that," replied Jack, patting the leg he'd injured in a bike accident several years earlier, "but I don't think I'm quite ready for a Harley yet either. Wouldn't mind a Beemer to go touring though. How do you fancy a week touring Europe next year?"

"With these new girls we are going to meet I suppose?"

"You never know your luck. We might even meet some on the way."

"Yeah, right."

"Have faith my friend," Jack reassured Mike as they walked on, "you never know what – or who – is just around the corner."

"I wish," grumbled Mike with a resigned look on his face.

Jenny and her parents found a table by the window of *Rosie's Coffee Shop*. The little café was set back from the road and was certainly aimed squarely at the tourist trade with its snug and inviting *olde-worlde* charm. There was the warm aroma of comfort food that you know you shouldn't be eating but are somehow powerless to resist. As if that were not enough, the sight of home-made muffins, scones and other assorted temptations sealed the deal. What more could one ask for on a cold winter morning?

Jenny relaxed in the homely atmosphere, draped her coat and scarf over the chair back and looked at her parents. No matter what else let her down in life, they were always there; constant, supportive and reassuring. They had liked Tony; he was, in their view, sensible, responsible and a good choice as a life partner. He played rugby, was popular with his team-mates and had a good career, and of course, he loved their daughter.

Most of that was true but unfortunately Tony also had a temper; a bad temper, but her parents knew nothing of that and Jenny wanted to keep it that way. There was nothing to be gained by telling them; save to explain why they were no longer together. But Tony had made that part easier when he decided to accept a posting to Thailand which was where he was spending Christmas this year; no doubt in the company of some teenage bar girl who he could employ to satisfy his fantasies as he had wanted to with Jenny. She was certainly no prude and very open-minded when it came to their love life, but some of Tony's *preferences* were rather too much even for her. Her refusal to indulge in some of his more extreme fantasies had been one of the things that had caused him to become aggressive. Although she was still smarting from his departure, realistically she knew she was better off without him.

The coffee and chocolate muffins arrived and broke her daydream. "Mmm, this looks good," she muttered as she bit into the soft cake. Chocolate was a great anaesthetic for emotional pain.

Mike and Jack wandered slowly through the streets, stopping occasionally to check out the art or antiques in the Dickensian windows of the ancient shops.

"Fancy a coffee?" asked Mike.

"Why not? Let's find somewhere that does food too. I wouldn't mind a bite to eat."

Rounding the next corner they were assaulted by the agreeable aroma of fish and chips. They looked at each other ... "No," they chorused, and continued past the small shop, ignoring the fingers of temptation that reached out and beckoned them inside like the Sirens of the sea.

Jenny caught her reflection in the window of the coffee shop. She had never understood why she was considered pretty; she'd always thought of herself more as tomboyish or gamine. Her hair was cut shortish in what she described as a *pageboy dragged through a hedge backwards* style. Her teeth were a little wonky, although everyone said she had a lovely smile. She was blessed with high cheekbones, blue-grey eyes and a fair complexion, even if recent events had bestowed on her a few extra lines around her eyes. She usually dressed in a manner unlikely to attract attention although beneath her modest attire there was a well-proportioned and feminine figure. She grimaced at her reflection; maybe she should be a little less hard on herself; she'd seen a lot worse.

"So where are we going to meet these potential pillions," asked Mike as the two friends sat at a plain metal table awaiting their coffee in a small bakery shop on the main street. He absent-mindedly played with a sachet of sugar.

"Who knows? But I am going to get out more in the next year. You certainly won't meet anyone sitting at home by yourself, that's for sure. Then again, the woman of your dreams could walk through that door in the next five minutes."

They were interrupted by the waiter who brought their coffee and two filled baguettes.

After he left, Jack continued, "Strange saying that; *the woman of your dreams*. What or who would be the woman of *your* dreams?"

"I have no idea. I'd probably settle for female, human and breathing after all this time on my own," said Mike with a laugh. "How about you?"

"Good question. You know, I'm not convinced that it's a physical thing. Look at the last three girls I've dated; as disparate as it's possible to be."

"Desperate did you say?"

"Cheeky sod. No, disparate – you know, chalk and cheese. I mean Gemma was a perfect English Rose; tall, fair-skinned, blonde and blue-eyed. Hannah was a petite Singaporean girl; pale skin, very dark eyes, straight dark hair. And then there was Luisa, the striking olive-skinned Brazilian with hazel eyes and long curly hair. You can't get much more diverse than that."

"So which did you prefer?" asked Mike who had been hungrily stuffing his beef salad baguette into his mouth.

"I don't know, they all had their good points – and a few bad ones too. But that's my point; it wasn't just a physical thing. They were, to me, all beautiful in their own way, but it was deeper than that, there was something, a connection between us, you know?"

"Yeah, I know. I used to look for the perfect physical specimen but now I just want someone who understands me and will accept me for who I am. Like I said, female, human and breathing ... even barely breathing would be a start!"

Jack laughed, "You are such a daft sod at times. Have faith my friend, you're not such a bad catch. She is out there somewhere, I guarantee it."

Mike looked at his prematurely greying friend of thirty years. "I know; she's out there somewhere and I'm sat in here with an ugly bugger like you."

"Oh I give up," replied Jack with a shake of his head and bit into his tuna sandwich.

Feeling suitably revived by the coffee and muffins, Jenny, Ellen and Ted had emerged from the warmth of *Rosie's* and into the chilly wind that was blowing up through the town from the harbour. They pulled their collars close and Jenny slipped her hands into her coat pockets. Although she wasn't keen on the cold weather, it was certainly a beautiful morning. The sky was clear and a fresh salty tang filled the air as the wind whipped off the English Channel. Seagulls spiralled overhead as they searched for easy pickings in the seaside town. An art shop caught her eye and she stopped to look wistfully at a large oil on canvas depicting the view of Florence from the Piazzale Michelangelo high above the city; Brunelleschi's iconic terracotta dome of the beautiful cathedral dominating the Florentine skyline. Jenny had always loved this view of Florence and had promised herself that one day the repressed artist inside would make the trip to that most beautiful of cities, and maybe even pick up a paintbrush again.

"You OK love?" Ted asked his daughter as she emerged from her Tuscan daydream to find herself back in a chilly English seaside town in December. She smiled, noticing her mother some way up the street looking back at her.

"Sorry Daddy, I was miles away."

"Don't blame you. I bet it's warmer over there," Ted said supportively, noticing the painting. "Why don't you go? You know you'd love it there?"

"Just what I was thinking," she agreed, "we'll see." She linked her arm through Ted's and they continued walking to where Ellen was waiting patiently, just beyond a small café on the opposite side of the street.

Mike was just swallowing a mouthful of coffee when he noticed a very cute blonde passing outside the window. Jack noticed the expression on his friend's face change and turned around to see what had attracted Mike's attention, but he could see nothing.

"What?" he asked Mike who was still gazing into the distance over Jack's shoulder.

"Oh, just a little cutie passing by, but we were a bit too young for that one. She was about thirty and her fella looked nearer sixty. I don't understand it; some guys have all the luck. What do you think he's got that we haven't?"

"Well he probably doesn't spend his Sunday mornings sitting in cafés having lascivious thoughts about girls walking past the window, you randy old goat," Jack teased.

Mike looked at his friend who was grinning at his own humour and knew that had they been sitting the opposite way around, Jack would have been the one making lecherous comments and Mike would have been berating him just the same. Not to be outdone, Mike replied in the only way he felt was appropriate at the time. "Bollocks," he said quietly and went back to drinking his coffee.

Jack smiled. "Charming!"

The bohemian streak in Jenny was always attracted to the little shops down by the harbour-side which sold anything from ship's lanterns to dried flowers, from woodcarvings to seashells. She and her parents happily mooched around the little buildings which were quiet in comparison to the high season when the constant noise and bustle of bodies made the whole shopping experience far more stressful than it was worth. This morning was different and she noticed herself beginning to relax. it had been a good suggestion by her mother to have this day out. Stepping outside one shop she saw another opposite which was selling, among other things, all kinds of arty paraphernalia and she found herself being drawn inexorably towards it. Ellen and Ted sauntered along slowly behind her, enjoying the sunny winter day.

"No, that's not it," Mike advised Jack who was holding up a bronze-coloured resin cast sculpture of a naked woman. "It's similar but I want to get one that matches the others that I've got."

"Well I think you're going to be out of luck here matey," said Jack as he surveyed the jumble of figurines that surrounded him. "I don't see anything else similar."

"No problem, it was just a long shot. Anyway, it gave you the chance to pick up a few chicks didn't it," Mike grinned. "Come on, let's go."

Jack raised his eyebrows and started to follow his friend towards the door. As he walked, a small silver bracelet caught his eye, very similar to one that he had once spent half a month's salary buying for Gemma, his former *English Rose* girlfriend. He stopped for a moment and then, smiling to himself, turned to follow Mike out of the shop. Mike was nowhere in sight but coming towards him was the most amazing face he'd ever seen. Time slowed; the young woman passing him looked angelic; almost ethereal; totally beyond comparison and as she wafted past him he was completely mesmerised, unable to move or to close his mouth. He was transfixed. Her eyes, despite having a tinge of sadness, were a sparkling blue and perfectly complemented the corn-gold of her short but windblown hair. As she passed him, the feint trace of a smile crossed her generous lips, although Jack felt this was a naturally alluring feature rather than something directed at him.

He could smell her fragrance but he couldn't place it; was there a hint of coffee? He watched as the vision of loveliness vanished through an archway at the back of the shop before he regained his composure. His stomach felt as it did when he stepped out of the aircraft door on his one-and-only parachute jump many years before. He noticed that his hands were shaking and damp. He needed some fresh air and walked on unsteady legs out of the door.

Mike was standing outside in the winter sunshine lighting a Hamlet cigar as Jack emerged from the shop. "Thought you'd got lost," he called, then noticed the look on Jack's face. "Are you OK mate?"

"I've just seen the most beautiful woman in that shop."

Mike peered through the doorway. "Really? Where?"

"You must have seen her. She must have passed you on your way out."

"Didn't see anyone – well, nobody special. Where is she now?"

"In there somewhere. Wait, you'll see her," Jack gushed as they stood outside the little shop. After five minutes there was no sign of the mystery woman. Jack was wondering if he had actually seen her at all. "I'm going back in," he announced. Mike just shook his head.

"OK, you flush her out and I'll make sure she doesn't escape," he grinned.

One minute later Jack was back outside. "I just don't understand where she went," he said, "she's not in there."

"I think you need a beer," said Mike, "and you can tell me all about her."

"I don't understand," Jack repeated dejectedly, looking back over his shoulder.

Jenny, entranced by the small art gallery tucked away on the first floor had made a decision. She *would* go to Italy and she would take her paints with her. A couple of weeks in late spring or early summer would be perfect, before the schoolkids invaded. She had very nearly failed to notice the handwritten sign to the gallery at the bottom of the stairs but this unplanned detour to see the artworks displayed in the little shop had made her realise that she too wanted to express herself on canvas; to immerse herself in her paintings like she used to. Yes, she was going to Italy and she was going for the right reason, for herself – the first thing Jenny had done for Jenny in a very long time. Her parents had followed her up the stairs and were standing together looking at a winter countryside scene that depicted the early morning winter sun bestowing a pink hue to snow-covered fields beyond a five-bar gate. It was so realistic that it made Jenny shiver. Stepping between them she rested her hands gently on their shoulders. "Mum, Dad, there is something I want to tell you."

"No, not beautiful in the way a model might be airbrushed beautiful, just the sweetest, loveliest face I have ever seen, with a smile that could melt the ice caps. Michael, I think I'm in love." Jack was having trouble finding the words to describe the vision he had seen; she was so much *more.* "She was exquisite, cute, adorable, but where the hell did she go? I see the woman I want to spend the rest of my life with and she just vanishes. Typical." He consoled himself briefly with a large swallow of his pint of London Pride ale.

"Probably not the most traditional way of finding a future wife but certainly original," Mike commented. "You see this beauty, she ignores you, you walk away and then she disappears. All in the space of two minutes."

"But, well ... well maybe this was just a sign, a sign that she is out there and I mustn't give up hope." Jack was struggling to make any sense of the brief encounter, but the romantic in him told him this was more than just a one-off passing of strangers. He had seen her for a reason; but what reason?

"Come on, drink up," said Mike, draining his own glass. "Time to hit the road."

"When we go back to the truck, let's go past those shops again," said Jack glumly. "You never know."

"OK, if you want to mate. As you say, you never know'."

Conversation was brisk in the Volvo. Now that Jenny had made her decision her excitement was tangible and her parents were genuinely delighted for her. Ellen in particular had noticed the sparkle that had returned to her daughter's eyes. This day out had certainly been one of her better ideas. From the back-seat Jenny's enthusiasm washed over Ellen and Ted, and talk was of the Ponte Vecchio, the Uffizi Gallery, Botticelli and, of course, Michelangelo's David. She may even fit in a visit to Venice, or Pisa, or ... Well the possibilities were endless.

To add to the atmosphere within the vehicle, Ted inserted a CD and the velvet tones of Mirella Freni and Luciano Pavarotti filled the air as they performed the love duet from the end of act one of Puccini's Madam Butterfly, Jenny smiled and relaxed back into the leather seat. She loved Puccini's music; it was so passionate and at the same time romantic. All that was needed now was spaghetti bolognese and a glass or two of Chianti when they got home and the mood would be complete – Ted had a similar idea.

The cab of the white Toyota was less musical but equally highly-charged with emotion. Jack just couldn't stop thinking about the girl he had seen but he was still mystified about her disappearance.

"You're really serious about this aren't you?" Mike asked. "What was it about this mystery girl and how come I didn't see her?"

"Good question. Do you believe in ghosts? I'm beginning to wonder if I really saw her or was just fantasising." Jack said, gloomily staring into the distance as Mike pulled out to pass a silver Volvo which was turning off the road and into the car park of an Italian restaurant just ahead of them.

***

Hey, Good Looking

She shook the wet tendrils of hair from her face; her surfboard cleaving through the foaming aquamarine wave as she used all her skills to battle, and to master, the extreme elements created by the clash of wind and water.

The agitated, sparkling, raging ridge of white water which had started life hundreds of miles from shore was now cresting, and just begging to be ridden; to be tamed.

Just below the surface, a dark shadow lurked, and the obsidian eye of the Great White followed its next meal …

***

Missed It

Sunday

Midtown Firehouse of Engine 54 / Ladder 4 / Battalion 9 on 8th Avenue, Manhattan.

Firefighter Vincent O'Halloran, a thirty-five year old Irish American with an easy-going charm and a boyish grin, playfully begged his good friend, Greg Mendez to swap his Tuesday morning shift with him.

"Come on buddy, help me out here would you?"

"Oh, I see. I have to leave my lovely Erin all by herself so that you can have fun with the beautiful Lara huh? Doesn't seem very fair to me."

"But you and Erin see each other all the time. Lara has been away for three weeks and she's flying in to JFK tomorrow afternoon, for a few days. I just want to make us a nice meal and catch up on all the news."

"Yeah, right," Greg replied with a mischievous grin, "a little R&R huh? Rest and Romance!"

"Oh, c'mon, you have time with Erin every day. Ours is more like having a long-distance relationship. Three weeks apart is a long time, I don't wanna just rush out the door as soon as she arrives, you know what I mean?"

"Yeah yeah, okay, I'm only joshing with you," Greg

responded jovially, "Of course I'll swap with you, as long as you clear it with Olsen."

Robert Olsen was a pretty easy-going guy and as the station had been fairly quiet lately, he readily agreed to the arrangement, as long as both shifts were going to be covered. He adjusted the complex shift roster accordingly, satisfied that the records were correct. As Vince and Greg left his office, Olsen called out cheerfully, "Have a good Tuesday guys."

Monday
JFK International Airport, New York.

"Ladies and gentlemen, welcome to New York's JFK Airport. Local time is 15.35 and the temperature is a pleasant 72 degrees.

For your safety and comfort, please remain seated with your seat belt fastened until the aircraft has come to a complete stop and the Captain has turned off the 'Fasten Seat Belt' sign.

Please check around your seat for any personal belongings you may have brought onboard with you and please use caution when opening the overhead bins, as heavy articles may have shifted around during the flight.

On behalf of Delta Airlines, Captain Byrne and the entire crew, I'd like to thank you for joining us on this flight and we look forward to seeing you on-board again very soon. We wish you a safe onward journey to your final destination. Have a nice evening."

With those words, Cabin Services Director, Lara Garcia closed the intercom and prepared for disembarkation at New York's Kennedy airport, after a lengthy itinerary which had included long-haul trips to Europe, the Middle-East and South America.

Lara was a popular thirty-two year old, her striking looks evidencing her Argentinian heritage. She was slim but shapely, her long wavy hair was worn up when she was working and, somewhat unusually for a Latina, and adding a touch of the exotic, she had beautiful grey/blue eyes. She smiled easily and genuinely, even when rhythmically greeting her two hundred and forty-odd passengers boarding the Boeing 767 which served as her regular workplace.

Lara and her crew were all fatigued and looking forward to spending a few days in New York. Although she was friendly with others in the crew, she wouldn't be staying with them in the hotel on this stopover. New York was her hometown and she was happy to be back and to be able to spend time with Vince, her boyfriend of almost two years.

As the last of the passengers disembarked from the aircraft, Lara went through her end-of-flight routine checks and finished writing her flight report before grabbing her Travelpro carry-on bag and leaving the aircraft with the rest of her crew. Leaving the others to board the crew bus taking them to their hotel, Lara cleared the airport by 5pm, grabbed a cab to Jersey City and let herself into Vince's apartment, with its commanding view of the Hudson River and Manhattan, which she had just crossed on her way in from JFK. The apartment had been bought with a sizeable inheritance from Vince's wealthy grandfather and was considered prime real-estate.

Vince may have been a strapping firefighter but he was also a romantic at heart and had the table set and added flowers in a crystal vase. A bottle of Chilean Sauvignon Blanc was chilling in an ice bucket and he was pottering in the kitchen, expertly preparing his speciality rich seafood pasta sauce. Lara went up behind him, wrapped her arms around his waist and kissed his neck. "Something smells good" she whispered.

He put down the wooden spoon, turned, took her in his muscular arms and they kissed eagerly and comprehensively. "Good trip around the world honey?" he half-joked.

"Tiring, I really need this break and some decent sleep. I must be getting old." She removed the clips holding her hair up and shook it loose, the dark waves falling around her shoulders.

"You look pretty good for an old lady to me," Vince smiled, "but I know just how you feel."

"Oh c'mon, you're not too shabby either."

"True, and I'm a pretty good cook too."

She slapped his arm playfully.

"Ow, you brute," he teased, feigning pain, "I'm going back to slave over my hot stove."

He pulled away to tend to his sauce and pour them both a glass of wine. They chatted happily for a short while before she declared that she was going for a quick shower and to change out of her uniform; something which for Vince is always tinged with a little regret. It was the sight of her in uniform that had first attracted him to her ... well, partly.

They had first met in a grocery store when Lara had stopped off to buy supplies after she had returned from a flight. Nothing special about that; however Vince had been totally captivated as, dressed in her smart uniform, she almost seemed to dance, lost in thought along the aisles. He had been unable to take his eyes off her swaying hips which moved rhythmically and unconsciously to the salsa music playing throughout the store. He was entranced, and she also soon noticed the tall, handsome firefighter smiling at her. They were powerless to resist the inevitable outcome ...

As Vince knew only too well, Lara loved all kinds of Latin music and the song coming from the CD player was *Bésame Mucho*, a romantic Latin bolero by the Dominican singer Maridalia Hernández. Hearing the soft romantic tones, Lara said softly, "You really are such a lovely man," and she did exactly as the song suggested and kissed him again, before heading for the shower and a change into more appropriate clothes.

"What do you think?" she asked as she sashayed back into the kitchen after her shower, wearing a pretty floral summer dress which swished elegantly as she walked, and showed her legs off to perfection.

"Wow, you look stunning. Get over here!"

She pouted and shook her head, "Nope, you come here," she teased.

The dress had had the desired effect. Vince took her in his arms and held her close. "I'm trying to make us a nice dinner and you are distracting me," he joked with mock indignation.

"Well, if that's how you feel ..."

He kissed her on the nose, "Now be a good girl and sit at the table, dinner is about to be served."

"But I though you liked bad girls," she quipped with a grin.

"Later," he said, turning her around, guiding her to the table and patting her shapely rump, "Sit!"

"Oh, OK mi amor," she sighed good-naturedly as she sat at the table and looked forward to her first home-cooked meal for several weeks.

They both switched off their cellphones: neither was on-call that night and they didn't want any distractions to spoil their romantic reunion. The garlic-rich but delicately-spiced seafood dish was a triumph, perfectly complimented by the chilled Sauvignon and they relaxed into the early evening, gazing out across the Hudson towards Lower Manhattan as a massive thunderstorm flashed and grumbled overhead. They snuggled cosily on the sofa, opened a second bottle of wine, flirted gently and enjoyed getting close again after their three weeks apart.

Unsurprisingly, the inevitable soon became irresistible. He took the empty wine glass from her hand and they retired to the bedroom to finally make up for lost time.

Tuesday
Vince's apartment in Jersey City.

Around 6:00 am the next morning, Vince got out of bed and stole a glance out of the window to see that the thunderstorm had passed and a fine clear morning was in prospect. He pulled the curtains closed again and got back into the warm bed. He snuggled closely into Lara who moaned gently but didn't wake. Within five minutes, Vince had also fallen back into a deep comfortable sleep. They were both dog-tired after working long, busy hours, too much wine the night before and, in Lara's case, the exhausting effects of jet-lag after her long-haul flights. And both were completely oblivious to the unusually frenzied background cacophony of Police sirens outside.

By 10:00 am, across the Hudson, the South Tower of the World Trade Centre had collapsed and Firefighter Greg Mendez and many of his co-workers were entombed beneath it.

Around forty minutes later on that fateful Tuesday morning, Vince finally stirred, kissed Lara's bare shoulder, padded sleepily to the window and threw back the curtains on a fine, crisp fall day – perfect: apart from the cataclysmic scene which met his unbelieving eyes. A pyroclastic cloud completely blanketed Lower Manhattan and the huge pall of dark grey smoke climbed imposingly above the Statue of Liberty into the clear blue sky from where Twin Towers had formerly dominated the iconic skyline. It looked just as though a volcano had erupted outside his window.

"Oh Jesus, I can't believe it. What the hell? Lara. Wake up!"

Lara opened one eye as she dragged herself unwillingly from the arms of Morpheus. "What is it? What's happened?" she mumbled, her head still full of sleep. She rubbed her eyes and stretched. "What is it baby?"

The usually unflappable firefighter was suddenly panic-stricken. His first thought was to call the Firehouse and find out exactly what had happened, but all the cellphones were dead: no signal anywhere. Lara joined him at the window and her eyes widened as she took in the apocalyptic sight before her. "What the hell's happened?" she muttered, as a sudden light-headed sensation flowed over her and caused her to crumple silently to the floor.

"Lara? Are you OK honey?" Vince asked, kneeling beside her and supporting her in his arms.

Lara looked up, took a deep breath, refilling her lungs and immediately felt better. "Just help me up, please."

Vince lifted her easily and tenderly to her feet and

guided her to a chair before fetching her a glass of water. "Better?"

"I'm OK, I just fainted. It must be the shock of seeing that sight before I was fully awake." Her first-aid training kicked-in, "My blood pressure probably dropped from getting up too quickly; I'll be fine now. But Dios mío! What did we miss?"

They were both drawn inexorably back to the horror unfolding before their eyes. Vince switched on the TV, and little by little they heard the unbelievable account of what had unfolded that morning as they both slept peacefully and unwittingly in their bed.

"Babe, are you sure you will be OK? I really need to get to the firehouse, they're gonna need all the help they can get."

"I understand honey, I'll be fine. You go, but for God's sake take care. Who knows what you might find when you get there?"

Vince jumped in his truck and tried desperately to make his way to the Firehouse. But every road to Manhattan was either gridlocked with traffic or closed-off by the Police. Sirens were blaring everywhere and the pall of dark smoke overshadowed the whole skyline. It was total chaos and finally he turned back for home in frustration.

The news on every radio station was confused. Shock, disbelief, refusal to accept. The most dire reports and potential casualty statistics – most of them pure speculation at this early stage – but horrific in their possibilities.

What Vince couldn't possibly have known was the true devastation suffered by his own firehouse that day.

Engine 54 / Ladder 4 / Battalion 9 in Midtown suffered the greatest loss on September 11th 2001. Fifteen of its members died that day – more than any other firehouse in the city. No single firehouse was hit harder.

Fifteen men – everyone working that shift – raced to the World Trade Centre and never returned.

Epilogue

In June 2002, Lara gave birth to a baby boy who would be named Gregory; conceived unexpectedly in a tender moment of love, just twelve hours before his namesake perished brutally but instantly beneath the thunderous rubble of the once-magnificent South Tower of the World Trade Centre.

The world would never be the same again.

***

Don't Forget your Toothbrush

"How about Saturday?"

"Well I have a show but you're welcome to come with me."

"Hmm … not really sure it's my thing but hey, why not?"

Soon after that conversation, Graham found himself standing beside an ageing and much-used blue Land Rover and matching horsebox in a muddy, but rapidly-drying field on Romney Marsh, as what appeared to him to be a huge and feisty horse was led gently out of the box.

Graham was not a horse-lover. As far as he was concerned they were dangerous things; one end bites, the other kicks, and there are no brakes. No, the only reason he was there was because the current object of his romantic ambition was a total horse-fanatic who was taking part in a cross-country and show jumping event aboard the huge chestnut beast, snorting and standing tall before him. The things you'll put up with at the beginning of a relationship just for the vague prospect of a night of passion!

He had first spoken to Anna on the phone, flirted with her and they'd become curious enough to meet each other.

She was very much a country girl, ruddy-faced with a mane of ever-tousled blonde hair and a fine line in wellies and body warmers. Not really his usual type but secreted beneath that outfit, he was convinced, was a body to die for; what other incentive did he need? Besides, he couldn't help but notice that she scrubbed up pretty well in her jodhpurs and riding boots too.

This was their second date. They had first met two weeks earlier in a pub near Lydd, close to where she worked at the airport for an executive-jet charter company. Graham still couldn't quite picture her in the smart uniform, dealing with very well-to-do clients as he contemplated the undeniable appeal of her jodhpur-clad derrière while she endeavoured to fit the bridle to the evermore belligerent horse whose head was a good twelve inches higher than hers. He smiled to himself. It had been a fairly instant mutual attraction when they met, mainly physical but helped along by their shared love all things fast and dangerous: cars, aeroplanes; and for her, horses; for him, motorcycles. Strangely she had never been on a bike and there was no way he would ever get on a horse; although that was something she had already told him she was planning to cure today. He, on the other hand, didn't think so.

After fifteen minutes of struggling and cajoling, Anna was finally happy that all the relevant leather items, of which, it seemed to Graham, there were far too many, were in the appropriate positions and sufficiently tightened to ensure she didn't end up on the floor. To Graham, horses were a little like sailing boats; too much effort involved for too little return. But each to their own.

The field was now filling with country types and Graham felt distinctly out of place in his jeans and leather jacket amongst the sea of flat caps, tweed and Barbour. Even the local vicar, his dazzling white dog-collar, eye-catching in the early summer sunshine and with a wreath of pipe smoke, halo-like around his head, was chatting enthusiastically with several of the competitors.

"Come on you," said Anna, grabbing Graham by the hand, "We're going to walk the course," and she led him off in the direction of a gate in the hedge that led to the woods beyond. "It might be a bit muddy but we can soon throw your jeans in the washing machine when we get back," she added with a wink.

Muddy, it turned out, was an understatement and they both needed to wash off their footwear in a bucket of water when they returned.

But Graham was impressed. The fences that Anna would be jumping on the cross-country section seemed to him both huge, and hugely dangerous. Add to that, the fact that the horse was considerably taller than she was and all in all, he was convinced that she was very slightly crazier than he'd realised, something which actually he found very appealing.

Even more impressive was that when she returned from her first round she had incurred no penalties. Her delight was evident from the unexpectedly passionate kiss he received when she finally slid down from the steaming, puffing beast. The horse seemed less able to express its delight appropriately and promptly provided the local gardeners with a good bucket-load of fine rose manure, right next to Graham's boots. Anna laughed and put her arms around his neck. "What do you think of your first horse-show so far?" she giggled.

"Smellier and dirtier than bikes."

"Me or the horse?"

"Well – both actually!"

She slapped him playfully. "You can buy me a coffee for that while I give Tosca a rub down and get changed. Go!" she commanded with a pout and wiggled off provocatively into the horsebox.

The afternoon passed equally well for Anna. Now looking far more elegant in her show-jumping jacket, newly polished boots and with the wild hair netted tidily under the smart black crash hat, she managed to finish the day as the winner in her class.

After the prize-giving was completed and both Tosca

and the winner's rosette were positioned safely back in the horsebox, Anna hauled Graham to the opposite side of the field where several youngsters were gamely learning the basics of the sport on Shetland ponies. "Come on then, now it's your turn," she teased, poking him in the ribs and dragging him towards the tiny creatures.

"No thanks," he answered.

"Oh come on, even you can't fall off one of those."

"Wanna bet? No thanks, I'll stick with bikes and leave this brave stuff to you."

"Chicken! Oh well, I hope you enjoyed your day anyway," she asked hopefully.

"I had a great time, and you were amazing. I was really impressed," he replied honestly.

"Well thank you kind sir," she smiled. "Okay let's get on our way. We still have work to do before we can shut the door of the stables and go home. I'll see if I can dazzle you with my cooking too and then we'll see whether you can do anything to impress me." She grinned cheekily, "I hope you remembered to bring your toothbrush."

Graham smiled back. "That's the nicest breakfast invitation I've had for a long time."

***

Tommy's Christmas

It's cold. I'm cold. This is no way to spend Christmas. I wonder when it will be a normal Christmas again, and whether I'll still be around to see it.

At least it's quiet here tonight and the stars are bright. Actually, if you can have such a thing in this filthy godforsaken place, it's a really beautiful night. This is the first quiet one we've had for God-knows how long and, despite everything else it actually feels, well, almost Christmas-like.

I wonder what Mum and Dad are doing right now? And Jim, I bet he's looking forward to tomorrow's roast dinner; what I wouldn't give for some of that. But with luck we'll get some cake or plum pudding and maybe even a little extra rum ration. It won't be anything like the Christmas we'd have at home, but compared to our usual trench rations it will seem heavenly.

The moon's coming out from behind the scattering of clouds, that'll make life interesting; it's almost like daylight. Strange how at home, many people are afraid of the dark and yet, here it gives me a sense of security. Even so, I'd better keep my head down. I know, a letter home would be good while I'm in this positive mood, if I get these frozen fingers to work.

Dearest Mother, Father and Jimmy,

Just a quick note on this Christmas Eve to tell you that you are all in my thoughts and my prayers. It is a quiet and cold night here, there isn't a sound save for the crackle of ice on the puddles. But we are in good spirits and looking forward to coming home in the new year ...

Strange. I thought I heard singing, over there across the line. Yes, there it is again, they're singing a carol. It sounds like Silent Night.

Mother, Father; Fritz is singing Silent Night. And I can hear our lads too. I think it's the Welsh Fusiliers down the line, they are singing Good King Wenceslas and ... and they're all standing up, getting out of the trench. Now our lads are moving out too. There are lights, lanterns, and Jerry is waving small fir trees ... This is crazy. I have to go now, something amazing is happening in no-man's land. Someone has a football!

I'll write more tomorrow, God willing.
Your loving son, and brother,
Tommy

***

I'm Sorry

"I'm sorry." His first words to me on that dark morning ...

"I'm sorry love: come on sleepy-head, it's time to get up" he'd said. He shook me gently by the shoulder as I grunted at him and snuggled back into the warm embrace of the duvet. He kissed me softly on the forehead in his gentle, non-sexual way which still always made me feel so sexy, but before I could respond he was closing the bedroom door and I heard his footsteps padding down the stairs. Reluctantly I dragged myself up into a sitting position and fumbled bleary-eyed for the cup of tea he had brought me. I normally love a lie-in at the weekend so 4:00 am Sunday morning starts are not my idea of a fun weekend activity. Even so, thirty minutes later I was showered, dressed and ready to support my man for his weekend quest to be the best. I pulled on my coat and boots, made one final check that everything was switched off and pulled the front door closed. It was time to go.

Outside, Gary was making his ritual final check on the already double-checked straps which secured his pride & joy to the trailer. The big yellow and white Yamaha sporting a large number 34 on the front and either side of the fairing glistened beneath the street lights with its fine sheen of droplets that drizzled from the early morning clouds – a passing shower, no more.

"Ready?" he asked when he heard me behind him.

"As ready as I ever am to go out in the rain at this time of the night," I teased him.

He smiled. "Have I told you that I love you?"

"Not this morning."

"Well I do. Now get in the car woman and let's be on our way."

I stuck out an inch of pink tongue and poked him in the ribs with my finger as I squeezed my breasts unnecessarily closely as I passed him and made my way around to the passenger side of the car. He resisted the temptation and two minutes later we were on our way ... His mind was on other things today.

Gary had been racing bikes since before I met him; in fact we'd been introduced by a girlfriend of mine from college whose brother had also been a bike racer. There had been no instant attraction; although he was undeniably a good-looking guy, I'd initially thought him selfish and verging on arrogant, but it was this determination and self-belief that had brought us to this moment. He was on the verge of securing his first championship. We weren't talking World Championships here; he was no Barry Sheene, but nevertheless, to be the best in Britain against some really serious competition was no mean feat. He had worked hard, first to finance his racing and secondly to prepare the bike into the fast, reliable machine now trailing along four feet from our rear bumper.

He was quiet this morning; self-absorbed; focussed. It was to be one of the biggest days of his life. I didn't intrude with small talk.

It was almost 7:30 when we pulled into the circuit. The sky had cleared and the morning was bright but chilly. Puddles covered the paddock as we splashed through to find a dryish spot to set up camp for the weekend. Many riders had arrived the night before but we managed to find ourselves a spot which was flat, solid and dry, close to the other guys who raced with Gary. We had arrived for this all-important weekend.

I'd been going to race meetings with Gary for long enough to know how the day would pan out and what my role would be. You could usually tell the experienced girls; they were the ones who didn't hang around too closely to their man. I knew to give Gary his space. He, like most of his mates, was not really very good company on race day, especially one as big as this. There was too much for him to think about without having me to worry about as well.

The racing fraternity are a close-knit group and when the circus meets up every couple of weeks or so: it is a gathering of friends and rivals. Over the years, we all get to know each other and friendships are formed so I was happy to wander off and find some familiar faces while Gary unloaded the bike, signed on at Race Control and chatted to the other guys who he'd be racing against later in the day.

Almost immediately I bumped into Barbara; slim, petite and unfairly bosomed, she was generally known around the ever-macho paddock as *Sex on Legs*. Her fella, Paul, was one of Gary's closest friends and most-feared rivals for the title.

"Hi Sarah, fancy a coffee?" she called, noticing me pulling up my collar against the chill of the Norfolk morning.

"If you're buying, I'm drinking," I replied and we shuffled off towards the café.

As we entered, the humid air suffused with the waft of bacon wrapped itself around us and thoughts of the chilly morning were left outside the door. In spite of the temptation in the air, we resisted the urge to tuck into the full English and just made do with the coffee. Barbara paid and we settled ourselves by the window and watched as the paddock slowly blossomed into life outside the steamy glass.

I liked Barbara. She didn't seem to take life too seriously. Of course, what the boys did was definitely risky but she loved the racing, she knew everyone, flirted outrageously with all the men and gossiped with the girls. And the gossip varied from the often-complicated love lives of the riders, all high on testosterone when not high on adrenaline, to the relative merits and failings of all the competitors in their riding techniques. Of course, today all talk was of the championship.

"You know, whatever happens this weekend, our two are going to be impossible to live with afterwards don't you? Paul is so up for this he's been a real pain in the arse for the last three weeks. How's Gary; did you give him his *breakfast of champions* this morning?" she enquired with a wicked grin.

"Certainly not," I answered with mock indignation, "He's got to earn it first."

"Treat 'em mean, keep 'em keen huh?"

"Well they reckon it works with us don't they? Actually, Gary's been so focussed on this weekend, he hasn't been very interested lately."

"I know the feeling. Bloody frustrating isn't it?" she grumbled. "Still, plenty of time for either a celebration or a consolation shag next week eh?"

Outside the window, the circus had come to town. Heroes, helpers and hangers-on were all hard at work, preparing bikes, cleaning riding gear, checking tyres and all the hundred and one other things which need to be checked, adjusted and fixed before anyone is allowed to take to the track. We finished our coffee and made our way slowly back to where the lads were busy winding each other up about who was going to win the championship, but underneath the banter, I could see that each was deadly serious in his determination. There were just two more races to go and by the end of today, the championship would be decided. Somebody would leave very happy and two others would be seriously disappointed, and of course, I wanted my man to be the happy one.

There were three lads in with a chance of winning the big prize; Gary, Paul and *Kamikaze* Kevin Anderson, as he was known. I wasn't worried about Gary and Paul. They had been racing close, hard but fair all season but Kevin; he troubled me. He had made a few questionable moves and had a couple of big crashes this year, but had battled back to still, just, be in with a chance of taking the title. The problem was, he was young; still only eighteen and, as with so many eighteen-year-olds, he thought he was invincible. Lots of the other guys had talked about him being an accident looking for somewhere to happen, and they all hoped he didn't happen anywhere near them. Today was no exception. Gary's friend, Andy, came over to join us.

"Just had a word with *Kamikaze Kev* and tried to talk some sense to him. I actually think he sees his reputation as his best chance to win; intimidation is his best weapon and he knows it."

I could sense the hackles rising on the back of Gary's neck, and I swear Paul's chest puffed up in indignation.

"Well, he's not bloody intimidating me," huffed Gary.

"Cocky little shit," grumbled Paul.

Barbara and I both knew better than to get involved in these '*my dick's bigger than your dick*' arguments so we left the boys to it and wandered off to find some decent girly conversations to join in with …

The sun came out and slowly, the dampness of the morning began to evaporate, and as the air temperature rose, so did the atmosphere around the boys. The bikes had by been given the all-clear by the scrutineers and it was now time for practice. Gary had changed into his leathers and was pacing nervously. I sat, half in the car, my legs dangling outside, and polished the visor on his crash helmet. The PA system crackled into life: "*Attention paddock, attention paddock. All riders for practice session 5; solos up to 1300cc, please make your way to the collecting area.*"

I finished cleaning the visor and carefully stood the helmet on the roof of the car. Gary zipped up his leathers and pushed the bike off the stand. As always, my job was to clear up the 'debris' and stow everything away safely. He fired up the engine on the big Yamaha and I hugged him and gave him a final kiss before he pulled on the crash helmet which would transform him from my handsome husband into an anonymous gladiator; a contender for the title of 1300cc Superbike Champion.

"Good luck" I managed, and he winked at me before he

threw his leg over the bike, pulled in the clutch, clicked it into gear and accelerated away towards the collecting area. I picked up the stopwatch, made sure I had a pen and pad and locked the car. Barbara was heading toward the pit wall with Marielle, Andy's French girlfriend. He seemed to have a preference for foreign girls; this was his third in as many years. I jogged off to join them and watch our boys do their thing in timed practice ...

Twenty minutes later Gary was back in the paddock and he was not a happy boy ...

When I got back from my vantage point, the Yamaha was carelessly leant up against our car looking slightly the worse for wear and Gary was nowhere to be seen. He'd immediately stormed off to have words – many I imagined beginning with 'F' – with Kevin Anderson who had made a totally unnecessary and imprudent bullying move on the slowing-down lap and crashed into Gary's bike, snapping the front brake lever and twisting the clip-on handlebar in a northerly direction, Gary was lucky to stay onboard but was fuming at the potentially catastrophic move.

Thirty minutes later, I could see that Gary, usually pretty happy-go-lucky, was still furious as he sat quietly making the repairs to the bike. Paul, Andy and several more of their mates were all standing around and all disgusted with Kevin's recklessness. They were not the only ones who had noticed. The PA system squealed discordantly into life:

"Attention paddock, attention paddock. Rider of bike number 77 in practice session 5; Kevin Anderson, please report to the Clerk of the Course in the control tower."

Repairs finished and mood improving a little, I tried to take Gary's mind off the incident. "Come on love, let's go and get something to eat,"

"Good idea. Actually, I could murder a bacon sarnie and a cuppa,"

"Me too," and I took his hand as we headed for the café. He squeezed mine and smiled back at me.

As we walked off, elsewhere in the paddock, Kevin was seemingly untroubled. Acting with his usual impudence and without any shame or embarrassment after Gary's furious expletive-laden rant and accusations of incompetent stupidity. Even the call to visit the Clerk of the Course didn't seem to have fazed him. He really was an egotistical prat.

Kevin's disrespectful and indifferent attitude to the incident had also infuriated the officials. This wasn't the first time he'd been *'up before the beak'*, and this time Kevin was given a formal warning. Any further incident today would lead to automatic disqualification, and that would take away any chance of he had of winning the championship. Of course, all this only served to raise the tensions even more ...

Just before 1:30 it was time for their first race for the championship to get underway. The second was scheduled for 3:45 if the programme ran to time with not too many incidents or red flags delaying proceedings. Barbara and I watched from the pit wall as the grid formed up with Gary and Paul both on the front row and *Kamikaze Kev* two rows behind them. Our boys both looked across and gave Barbara and me the thumbs-up. Barbara gave Paul a wave and I blew Gary a kiss, and saw his eyes smile inside his full-face helmet. The green flag waved on the gantry and they all set off on their warm-up lap, the last chance before the start to make sure the tyres were warmed up and the engine, gearbox and brakes were all working well. A minute and a half later all the bikes were back in the grid slots ready for the start.

A green flag waved from the marshal at the rear of the grid, the startline marshal at the front furled his red flag and pointed it towards the start lights on the gantry as he walked off the grid. First gear was selected, the engine notes rising, the red lights came on and three seconds later, blinked out. The race was on.

The cacophony of multi-cylinder engines caused both Barbara and me to cover our ears as the modern-day gladiators thundered off the line, and twenty-eight tormented masterpieces of Japanese and European engineering were sent screaming towards the first corner.

As the boys came round at the end of lap one, Paul was leading on his Kawasaki, Gary's Yamaha was close behind in third and I noticed Kevin's gaudy purple and fluorescent yellow Suzuki was back in about tenth place, mired among a gaggle of other bikes as is normal on a first-lap as they all try to make themselves some racing space. This was good news for our boys as they had far less traffic to fight with and could make their escape at the front ... I hoped.

As the race progressed, positions swapped and changed and by the end of lap eight with two laps remaining, Paul had pulled out a lead of around two seconds over Gary who in turn had a good margin back to the man now in third place, Norfolk local, Mick Simpson.

Next time round, I watched as the pack arrived at the final chicane which I could see off to my left. The first three went through with no problem and headed for the line to start the last lap. However, Kevin had made progress up to fifth place and was fighting for fourth. As they exited the chicane and onto the start-finish straight, his rival slid off right in front of him and Kevin had to take to the grass to avoid the fallen bike. With no grip on the grass, three of those following close behind powered past him by the time he got to the line. It was time for the last lap, but that proved to be somewhat of an anticlimax.

Paul had an untroubled win and punched the air as he passed the chequered flag. Gary had wisely decided on a safe second place and good points rather than risking a non-finish. Kevin however, desperate to stay in contention for the championship had managed to get himself back into sixth place which just about still gave him a fighting chance. It would all go down to the final race.

Barbara and I were happy to see our boys shaking hands and comparing notes when we got back into the paddock. Their first question to us, of course, was, "Where did Kev finish?"

"Sixth."

"So he's still in the title hunt?"

I'd already tried to work out all the permutations before we'd left home. "I'm pretty sure he will be, but I think he'll need to win and for you two to have a problem and both finish lower that fifth."

"Bugger, I was hoping he'd wouldn't still be in with a chance by this time. You know how desperate he'll be. He worries me."

"So just go out and beat him then," Barbara quipped. Paul playfully slapped her Lycra-clad bottom,

"Yep, it's just that easy isn't it?"

She hugged him, fluttered her eyelashes and whispered playfully, "Well you're good at most other things. What's the problem?"

"The problem my dear is this bugger standing beside me. He might want to win this bloody championship too."

"Excuses excuses," she shot back, and flounced off seductively into their awning.

With Kevin Anderson temporarily forgotten, Gary joined in the banter, "So I'll just let you win the race and avoid any further marital strife shall I? Would that work for you Paul?"

"That would be perfect mate, and I'll buy the beers. Cheers!"

"Dream-on sunshine. You should prepare yourself for further grief from the wench. Let battle commence," and, grinning, they high-fived each other.

"Boys will be boys," I muttered as the gathering broke up and everyone went off to fit new tyres, refuel and make final adjustments for the culmination of a hard-fought season ...

3:30pm and the main event was looming and Gary's confidence was high. He was leading the championship so if he won the race or finished ahead of the other two, he was champion. If Paul won, Gary could afford to finish third and still be champ. And now confirmed over the speakers by the circuit commentator, there was only one other contender. For Kamikaze Kev to win the championship, he had to win the race and for Gary and Paul to both finish lower than fifth. I smiled to myself that I'd got the maths right.

"Attention paddock, attention paddock. All riders for race 14; solos up to 1300cc, please make your way to the collecting area."

I proffered some well-meaning advice to my hero,

"Good luck babe, you can do this. This is your moment. Just remember, it's only a race, don't do anything silly". Gary just raised his eyebrows in fake exasperation, "Women!" and then he kissed me and whispered, "Actually Sarah, this is *our* moment." He zipped up his leathers, pulled on his crash helmet and fastened the strap securely. He wheeled the bike out of the awning, pressed the starter, winked at me and was gone, off to do battle once again. I went in search of Barbara and our vantage point on the pit wall.

The grid formed up noisily in front of us, Gary and Paul on the front row, Kevin just behind them on row two. This was it. As the boys always said, "When the flag drops, the bullshit stops."

Green flag at the back; red flag removed at the front; red lights on; red lights off: GO!

Gary got a flyer and headed off at the front of the chasing pack. Paul struggled to keep his front wheel on the ground and Kevin dropped a couple of places to some fast starters behind him. The stage was set.

Five laps in and there was a four-way scrap at the front before an over-keen Jim Richards high-sided over the handlebars at the final corner.

Gary was now leading and looking comfortable, but not complacent – he was never complacent. He had great respect for Paul, they had raced together for years, they had battled hard but fair throughout the season and would never put each other in a dangerous situation. They knew their limits, and as they flashed past for the penultimate time they had pulled a small gap on Kevin who was now up to third, however, it looked like it was going to be a two-way fight to the line.

But as they crossed the line to start the last-lap, the three adversaries went past us side by side, all tucked in behind the screens, chin on the tank and twist grips on the throttle-stop. The chasing group followed a comfortable two seconds behind them. Sensing a last-gasp opportunity to take the win, Kevin Anderson dived underneath Paul as they tipped the bikes into the first turn for the final time, but as always, it was ill-judged. His move was not only reckless and irresponsible but this time it would have far-greater consequences; greater than he could possibly have imagined. He had once again pushed too hard; his ambition had outweighed his talent.

In his desperation to get past Paul he had braked too late and as he clipped the inside kerb with his front wheel, it folded underneath him. He fell from his Suzuki which then set off a domino effect as it clattered into Paul's lime-green Kawasaki. That in-turn smashed at high speed into Gary who was thrown from his bike, straight into the path of the following pack of six riders who could do little avoid him.

Several riders crashed trying to avoid the stricken Gary who lay motionless on the track. But one rider, completely unsighted by the chaos unfolding in front of him, came upon Gary's inert figure too late, and despite his best efforts, at almost 90 mph, his bike's metal footrest struck Gary's helmet and violently spun him around on the tarmac. The race was immediately red-flagged and as soon as it was safe to do so, the marshals and medical staff instantly rushed in to assist the injured riders.

Kevin Anderson stood up, uninjured and calmly walked off back towards the paddock as Gary lay unmoving on the track. He didn't even look back. A visibly shocked Paul sat thirty yards away, head in hands, staring unbelievingly at the white bone poking through his green leathers: unable to move due to the compound fracture to his right tibia, the direct result of the initial impact from Kevin's riderless missile.

Of course, I had no idea about any of this at the time. I only found out the details several weeks later. Weeks when I had time on my hands.

On the day I couldn't actually see the disaster that had unfolded; it was over the brow of the hill. From the pit wall, all we could see was red flags being frantically waved, ambulances being dispatched, blue lights flashing to the scene. There was no access to the race commentary in the pit lane but if there had been, we'd have heard the animated reporting of the big crash, but in the confusion it was unclear exactly who was affected or how bad it was. It was only when we realised that Gary and Paul had both been involved did the foreboding feeling begin to rise in my stomach. I swayed unsteadily, gasped for breath and started sweating profusely, terrified of what might have happened. I grabbed Barbara's hand and we ran to the paddock office to get some accurate information about their condition.

Both boys, along with two other riders had been taken to the medical centre, where Barbara and I were eventually granted admittance after a near-hysterical shoving match outside with an overly-assertive official. He had tried, with good reason, to restrain us from what we might see if he allowed us through the doors. But with my rising sense of panic I had lost all rationality. I really should have apologised to him, but I never did: my mind was elsewhere. Finally, I was allowed in to see my unconscious husband. There was only so-much the circuit's medical team and their limited facilities could accomplish at the track so as soon as the boys had been stabilised, both Gary and Paul were transferred to Norwich Hospital for further urgent assessment and treatment: Gary by air ambulance and Paul following by road. As soon as she found out what had happened, Andy's girlfriend Marielle generously offered to drive Barbara and myself to the hospital so that we could be with them.

But when we arrived the news on Gary was not good, in fact it could hardly have been worse.

Gary had been quickly assessed and was already in the intensive care ward and connected to a ventilator. He had been placed in a medically induced coma to give him the best chance of recovery after suffering a severe trauma and swelling to the brain. The impact when the footrest clipped him as he lay on the track had been so extreme that his crash helmet had fractured and been knocked from his head. That caused his brain to violently impact the inside of his skull as his head struck the tarmac for the second time. Don't ask me how that is even possible but I knew I'd seen it happen once before, in a televised race he was watching. It was a sickening sight then, but now it was all too close to home.

As soon as I was allowed in to see him, I sat beside his bed. His mouth and nose were a snake's nest of tubes and my pent-up emotions overflowed. The dam broke and I burst into uncontrollable sobs as I held Gary's limp, but thankfully still warm hand, punctured by cannulas. Remarkably there was no visible sign of injury to his head or face, the damage was all internal.

He was in the coma for four weeks and during that time I never left his side. With Paul also hospitalised and under observation for the first week, I was lucky to have the initial support of Barbara who had also temporarily moved into a hotel in Norwich so she could be with him. Even after she and Paul had decamped back home to Essex to complete Paul's recovery, Barbara called me every other day with positive words and offers of support. She was a great friend but our lives had all been put on hold and nothing would ever be the same again.

The doctors did their best to remain positive; hopeful that Gary would make a good recovery and have a decent quality of life, but they also warned me that he would probably never be quite the same man again. They were over-optimistic ...

Although he partially recovered, his physical and mental capacity was greatly impaired and there followed months of rehabilitation, both physical and psychological. But almost as bad was his inability to communicate properly, and the efforts of several speech therapists had achieved little. His frustration was palpable.

For the next two years I did the best I could for Gary but his high level of disability made it so difficult to be effective. I felt helpless and, although it was clear that he still loved me, I felt unworthy of his love. His ongoing frustration at not being to do anything for himself, or even to get into the car so that I could take him away from staring at the same four walls everyday, or just having a normal conversation made it unsustainable. I started thinking about getting professional help and shamefully, I frequently drank a whole bottle of wine in an evening and cried myself to sleep.

My tear-filled eyes sometimes drifted over to the display cabinet filled with Gary's slowly tarnishing history of his racing successes. I stared at the substantial and elaborately decorated silver trophy which upstaged the collection. The trophy which I had accepted on his behalf while he was still in hospital. The trophy which bore the three-line inscription:

> *"British Aces Motorcycle Racing Club*
> *1300cc Powerbike Champion 2001*
> *Gary Anderson"*

Yes, Gary had been crowned 2001 champion in abstentia, and awarded the impressive trophy after all. Following a lengthy delay due to barrier repairs required after the accident, the fateful race had eventually been abandoned. Consequently, as Gary was still leading the championship at the time, the title was his. Despite my best efforts to explain, I'm still not sure whether he actually ever understood that ...

After a lengthy and comprehensive inquiry into the accident by the sport's governing body, Kevin's race licence was withdrawn and he was banned from ever racing in the UK again. He also needed some serious dental work after an "unnamed assailant" caught up with him one evening as he left the pub, called him a 'heartless bastard' and knocked his front teeth out with a single punch. I never saw or heard from Kevin Anderson; Gary's estranged, deranged and insanely jealous half-brother, ever again ...

Epilogue

I found Gary slumped in his wheelchair one Tuesday afternoon when I got home from work. As I threw my arms around his cold, lifeless body, I knew he was gone and my world crumbled around me. I felt just as dead as my lovely husband but unlike him, I was far from at peace. I sobbed uncontrollably. In his final battle, he had suffered his most crushing defeat.

Three arduous years after the accident, unable to come to terms with his shortcomings: totally frustrated by his inability to communicate properly and still relying on me for even the most basic of everyday tasks, a scattering of sleeping tablets and an empty bottle of scotch lay on the floor beside him. On his lap was a note pad and pen. On the pad he had scrawled just two words:

"I'm sorry"

***

Apocalypse

1:35am Saturday 26ᵗʰ April

They had to rest for a moment after attempting to carry their badly burned comrade to safety in this searing heat. They knew that sitting in this environment was the last thing they should be doing. With no protective clothing, every second they spent here was killing them; but despite the risk to themselves, they knew they couldn't just leave him behind ...

8:15am Friday 25ᵗʰ April

Yuri Zakharov pulled back the heavy curtains of the apartment he shared with his wife Irina and their five-year-old daughter Natalia, and looked out on a beautiful spring morning in the town of Pripyat. It was unusually warm for April, more like a summer day, and outside in the park, children were already running and playing in the sunshine. The twenty-eight-year-old was determined to make the most of this final day of his four-day break and enjoy some time with his young family, and with the weather like this, it was going to be perfect.

In the small kitchen, Irina was making coffee, breakfast, and preparing some food for a picnic later. Yuri came up behind her and encircled her slim waist with his arms. She nuzzled back into him and they kissed.

"Oh Mummy, don't dooo that," a small voice behind them exclaimed with all the mock indignation a five-year-old can muster. The parents both turned and laughed as Natalia stood in the doorway, hands on hips. Seeing them laugh, she smiled broadly and rushed towards them, arms raised for a hug.

Two hours later, the Zakharov family was wandering happily in the park, watching all the preparations for the forthcoming May Day celebrations. Pripyat was a good place for a young family to live, and today it was looking particularly resplendent in the spring sunshine, with the laughter of children and the early flowers all adding to the atmosphere. And most of all it was safe. Yuri and Irina had no concerns about Natalia as she ran and laughed with her friends. It really was a perfect day.

That evening as Yuri got himself ready for work, he felt sad. It had been a great day and now he was beginning a two-week shift of working nights. Not that his work as a technician at the plant was particularly taxing; it just kept him away from his beautiful wife and daughter for too long. He helped put Natalia to bed, kissed Irina goodnight and by 8pm was cycling the short distance to the plant to begin his shift in the Vladimir Lenin Power Plant's nuclear reactor Number Four.

Irina called the plant when Yuri had failed to return home on Saturday morning. She was assured by the dour automaton of a switchboard operator that everything was fine, Yuri was just required to work extra hours due to a special systems test. Irina wasn't unduly worried. This wasn't the first time Yuri had been kept back to deal with 'incidents' and she carried on with life as usual. Once again she decided to take Natalia to play in the park while the weather was still fine.

Despite all being injured in the initial blast, Yuri Zakharov and two colleagues had pulled themselves onto a ledge above the ruined reactor, determined to find a way to assess the damage. But by that time, it was already too late. Yuri and his fellow technicians would soon be the first to die from the lethal dose of radiation they received in the ten seconds they had gazed, transfixed above the blazing maw before they dragged themselves away.

8:00am Sunday 27th April

The town of Pripyat awoke on Sunday morning to the sound of a general alarm. The ever-secretive Soviet authorities were finally shamed into acknowledging the nuclear incident after instruments in Sweden detected the radioactive cloud heading west across Europe. Only now did they feel obliged to evacuate the town.

Yuri and his colleagues were so contaminated that they were buried in zinc coffins with the lids welded shut. Irina and Natalia, having spent an innocent Saturday inhaling and playing in the radioactive dust which covered the town, both became horribly sick and were also both dead within three months.

The fate of the Zakharov family, like thousands of other innocent victims, would be forgotten forever, due to the determination of the Soviet authorities to cover-up or destroy all medical records in the aftermath of the explosion of reactor number four at the Chernobyl Nuclear Power Plant at 01.23 am on Saturday 26th April 1986.

***

Near Enough

'Must pay more at attention to detail', his school reports had stated, but he didn't see why. He'd done alright by doing just enough, in fact he'd just been promoted to Workshop Supervisor.

The police cleared the wreckage from the carriageway, the charred bodies within, unrecognisable.

The inquest concluded, *'The brake union had been tightened incorrectly'*. A lack of supervision was blamed ...

***

Opening a Box

It felt to them as though reality had been suspended. The hospital which should have smelled of disinfectant; sterile, impersonal and innocuous, seemed dusty and neglected, its stained green and cream paint peeling from the walls. Bill and Helen followed the nurse through seemingly unending corridors with trepidation. The glare from the overhead fluorescents gave the depressing day an unnatural brightness, but that would never be enough to lift the enormous gloom that filled their hearts.

The past twenty-four hours since their arrival on the shell-shocked island had been an emotional roller-coaster of the most extreme kind. And before that, the phone call, the initial seismic shock wave that hit them, the unstoppable torrent of grief, the realisation that they actually needed to go to the scene and face the horrors of what they would find when they arrived. All of it was outside anything their previous life-experience could have prepared them for. They had no reference point, no ability to come to terms with what had happened, two and a half thousand miles from their normally comfortable and peaceful existence back home in Melbourne.

Finally they saw the sign they had been dreading; MORTUARY. Helen shuddered and gripped Bill's hand hard. What were they about to see? How could this be happening to them? The holiday in paradise had become a nightmare.

"Please ..." The Indonesian nurse smiled kindly and held open the door for them. Helen paused, unable to face what lay beyond that unforgiving threshold. Bill put his arm protectively around her shoulders. "Come on love, you know we have to do this."

Bill's heart was pounding too but, taking a deep breath, he placed his hand on his wife's back and tentatively, guided her through the open door.

They were met by the coroner, a fellow Australian who greeted them sincerely despite wearing the drained expression of a man who hadn't slept for several days. He led them into a side room; a cold, functional space that had clearly seen more than its fair share of emotion.

"First I want to tell you that your daughter didn't suffer," he began. His attempt at sounding reassuring was less than convincing. "There would have been no pain, no realisation of what had happened; it was instantaneous."

At this point the whole horror and reality finally struck the grieving parents. Ellie, their beautiful twenty-three-year-old daughter, on her first holiday alone had, in an instant, simply ceased to exist while enjoying a simple night out with friends during the long-awaited adventure she had dreamed of for so many months. They both collapsed into each other's arms in floods of tears.

"I know how difficult this must be for you," the coroner continued kindly, "but I'm afraid we really do need you to go through these formalities that will allow us to release Ellie's possessions to you.

Why? Why do we?" Helen demanded angrily. "This should never have happened," and she began to sob uncontrollably as she realised that Ellie must have been sitting at the table right next to where the bomb was hidden. "Bali was supposed to be a holiday paradise, not a bloody war zone. How could anyone be so callous; and for what? In the name of religion? What sort of vindictive god allows this to happen?"

Through the broken Venetian blind that hung lopsidedly at the window which linked this anti-room to the main section of the mortuary, Bill watched a white-coated orderly place a suitcase and a small box on a table. Her suitcase and a simple brown cardboard box which contained all that remained of his beautiful girl; her clothes and other personal belongings, which had been retrieved from her hotel room. The bomb had left little of the carefree young woman they had seen grow, develop and flourish. To add to their nightmare, it transpired that identification of Ellie's body had only been possible using dental records.

All that remained were the now-priceless valuables which had been left in the room for safety as she went out for her evening meal. The adornments which her grieving mother and father must now accept as the eternal reminder of their child, the beautiful daughter they would never see grow into a mature woman back home under the sunny skies of Melbourne.

"I can't do this Bill," Helen sobbed, "I just can't."

"I know love." He hugged his wife tightly. "Give us a minute would you Doc, we'll need a few moments before opening that box."

***

The Other Trench

I can't sleep. God in Heaven, I hate this war: mud; blood; rain; rats and lice. What a liberation it would be to have it all end tonight and to watch the sun rise tomorrow on something other than this stinking, sodden, filthy hole that has become my home, my whole world. Will I die in this godforsaken trench? Why should I live when all my friends are gone? And yet I want to live so much; to see a purpose to all this suffering; to tell my parents and my wife, and my children that I did it for them; I fought for our country; I survived this war to end all wars. I don't want those obnoxious swine the other side of this wood marching into my homeland, so I will fight alongside my comrades to win any extra fragment of this muddy, bloody battlefield until I can fight no more.

Who am I fooling? Children? My God, I am only nineteen years old, I didn't even get a chance to find a nice girl before this war started and we volunteered to defend both our freedom and our families. Of course, what we didn't know then was that we would still be fighting two years later. They told us it would be a swift victory; that we would crush the enemy; that they would put up little resistance, but that battle at Ypres changed all that. I had never seen such fury, violence and destruction, but now I see it every day; mutilation, dismemberment, and death. I don't just see it, I smell it, the stink of rotting flesh and shit is everywhere as the rain of shells unearth everything that we bury. And every night we wear death too. The blood and skin of our fallen comrades clinging to our uniforms as we doze for a few minutes at a time, afraid to lose consciousness too long for fear of what the rats might do to us.

It is strange, we are all going through all this together but I now only think in terms of comrades, fellow soldiers, they're not friends. The truth is, I hardly know any of the men I'm fighting with and I'm afraid to get close to anyone anymore because I know that within a few weeks at best, one or both of us will probably be dead. We share a smoke or a conversation but that is as close as I want to get. As we stumble over the barbed wire and rotting bodies out there, the last thing I want to see is the face of someone I care about looking up at me out of the sea of mud and filth.

It worries me that I am becoming immune to all this death and gore but it is everywhere, wherever you look there are bodies or parts of bodies. Some of these men will never again be anything more than a part of the landscape around this little French town of Arras, but I find it hard to care. All I want to do is to survive and go home from this filthy place to my parents' peaceful house in the hills, overlooking the river. What I would give to see that tonight, to drink wine and smoke a good cigar with my father, and retire to sleep in a real bed. Instead, I stand here, knee deep in mud; cold, wet and tired, my nerves shattered by the never-ending thunder of the big guns. At least we were not at the Somme; they say that it was even worse than here.

And what of my enemy? Is he, like me, too afraid to look out of the trench for fear of a bullet in the head? When we met our adversaries in no-man's land at Christmas during that first year of this awful war, they weren't demons. Probably we are not so different, he and I. He too fights for what he believes to be just. I am sure he too has hopes and dreams, family, and if he is lucky, a lover waiting and wondering.

The night is over; dawn is breaking. A whistle in the distant trench; my god, here they come again; charging into our guns just like they have so many times before.

Be strong Peter, it is time to be a soldier again: to defend your trench, to protect your family.

"God save the Fatherland. Come on Englanders, I am ready for you..."

***

Zeitgeist – A Sign of the Times

"Hey John."

"Oh hi Steph. Long time no see, how's things?"

"Pretty good thanks. Actually I got married recently."

"Really? Wow, that's great. I never thought you would."

"Thanks John. I didn't really expect it myself."

"Well I'm happy for you; congratulations. And is that Suzy Peterson coming this way? I haven't seen her for years either. She looks great."

"She certainly does. How do you know Suzy?"

"Actually we were engaged to be married many years ago."

"Oh really?"

"Yes really. Why, you look surprised Steph?"

"I am rather – because she's my new wife."

"Blimey ... Well, that could explain a lot!"

***

Betrayal

"You're damned right I don't understand. Explain it to me Brian; make me understand *exactly* why you betrayed me."

"Don't be like that, I only …"

Gemma exploded. "Don't be like that? Don't be upset that my husband has been screwing his pretty young colleague while I've been at home ironing his bloody shirts and taking care of his children. What the hell do you expect me to be like?"

"I just want to be open and honest about things."

"Open and honest? It's a bit late for honest don't you think?"

Brian moved towards her and raised his arms as if to hold her shoulders.

"Don't you *dare* touch me. Don't even think about it." She spat the words with such venom that Brian physically recoiled. "You have forfeited the right to ever touch me again Brian. Go to hell." With that she burst into tears and stormed out of the kitchen.

The house was silent. The shafts of sunlight slashed through the Venetian blinds like lasers as Gemma sat on the sofa, head in her hands, struggling to comprehend what she had just found out. Why hadn't she seen this coming? When the seed of doubt had been planted she had tried to dismiss the possibility by making excuses, looking for reasons not to believe what was unfolding in front of her. But it was his reaction when she had confronted him which really hurt her. He hadn't even denied it, he'd just lowered his eyes, unable to face her pain and said yes, it was true, he'd been seeing this bimbo; what was her name; Katie; and he was sorry that she had found out. Not sorry that he had cheated, not sorry that he had screwed the cheap tart, just sorry that Gemma had found out. The bastard.

And the bastard was now standing in front of her, holding a mug of tea … attempting to placate her with a goddamned mug of tea.

"Gemma?" His voice was pleading, pathetic. "Gemma, we need to talk." She ignored him and he moved to sit down beside her. "Here, have a cup of … Owww, shit; you bitch!"

Gemma had unintentionally timed it to perfection. As Brian was about to sit next to her she had managed to tip the whole mug of steaming liquid into his lap as she leapt to her feet, unable to bear his presence so close to her.

"Bitch; me?" she screamed. "I think you have the wrong woman my darling. I am your wife, the mother of your children, the one you chose 'till death us do part', remember?" He pushed past her, swearing and holding his groin. "I think the bitch is your little whore who will be mightily pissed off that you've burned your dick," she taunted as she pursued him into the bathroom where he was attempting to remove his steaming trousers and splash cold water onto the offended article. "How could you Brian? How could you do this to me and the kids?" As he reached for a towel, she punched him hard on the arm. That was her mistake. With the burning tea scalding his crotch and now the punch, Brian saw red and lashed out at his attacker.

The mirror dissolved into a thousand shards as her face smashed into it. For a second she was stunned before the blood ran into her eyes and she lifted her hand to try to staunch the flow. But something was wrong. It was as though she was touching a mask. She looked across at Brian whose face was registering shock. He could see what she couldn't, the large glass shard which had pierced her neck; and others sticking out of her bleeding face like some horrific red pin cushion. "Don't touch anything," he said. Her last memory of the event was slightly surreal; her cheating husband standing half-naked, speckled in blood and trying to look worried, as if he cared. Her head was swimming now; she felt sick, and the bastard was trying to hold her again ...

***

Jacob's Dream

Prologue

We all have a dream. Jacob was about to make his come true, although not quite in the way he had planned. Fate was to decree that a chance meeting would result in him not spending his retirement alone, nor in the way he had expected. And then ...

June 2001

Jacob had seen it all: tourists, locals, drunks and lovers; nothing fazed him. He waited patiently for the red light to change; his large leathery hands the colour of coffee, slowly drumming the steering wheel in time with Muddy Waters' classic *Mannish Boy* which emanated from the radio.

His mind wandered. Just a few more months and he would have saved enough money to achieve the goal he'd been working towards ever since Veronica had left him. It had taken fifteen long years to be sure he could comfortably escape this crazy city and change his life forever. The last thing he wanted was another woman in his life; his dream was simple: a boat, a small place on the beach and the freedom to fish quietly under the warm Caribbean sun. The toothy smile split his face as he pictured the scene in his mind. The light turned green and a nanosecond later, the horns began to blare. Yes, this was to be his reward for the fifteen long, cold winters as a New York Cabbie.

The following week however he would not be driving his cab. He was looking forward to a long weekend to indulge in one final pilgrimage to Chicago for the annual Blues Festival.

Jacob loved Chicago in the summer when it was warm. It may live up to its nickname of the *Windy City* as the arctic winds whip off the lake during the winter months but in the early summer sunshine it was such a vibrant place, full of life and music. As Jacob's flight approached over Lake Michigan and headed inland towards O'Hare International, the skyline, dominated by the gleaming black monoliths of the Sears Tower and the John Hancock Centre seemed to float past below him. He pressed his nose against the cold aircraft window and appreciated the lakeside scene through the oval frame. Despite the constant daily buzz of New York, he was really looking forward to the next four days in the city that never failed to impress and surprise him. He felt happy to be back.

The following day, Sam Prince was browsing in the travel section of a downtown Chicago bookshop. Dressed all in black, raven haired, wearing dark eyeshadow and lipstick he had immediately attracted the attention of the store owner who observed him suspiciously on the security monitor. The opening door agitated a small wind-chime dangling above as Jacob entered the store. A hardback copy of *Fishing the Caribbean* in the window had caught his eye on his way to the festival in Grant Park.

"Hi, how are you today?" enquired the store owner as Jacob closed the door.

"Good, thanks", replied Jacob,

"How can I help?"

"Yeah, that fishing book you have in the window …"

"Ah yes, good choice Sir," he interrupted, "Over there, near Count Dracula" he added caustically without lowering his voice, indicating towards Sam with a nod of the head. Jacob looked over to where the young Goth was standing and then back at the store owner who was grinning conspiratorially. *And I bet you don't like blacks either*, Jacob thought.

Finding the book almost immediately, Jacob flipped through the pages. The vibrant colours of the photographs in the book transported him back to his birthplace, and to the islands where he had spent his formative years; the same islands where he now planned to buy a small boat and enjoy his retirement years. Lost in his daydream, he was unaware of the dark figure closing on his right elbow.

"*Fishing the Caribbean*; that's awesome," commented Sam as they stood side by side, "Have you ever been there?"

Jacob nodded, "Long time ago," he said.

"I'm Sam," the dark figure stated, holding out his hand. Jacob looked up from the book at the shadowy bohemian figure standing beside him and smiling warmly. Jacob shook his hand warily, unused to this kind of friendliness back in New York.

"Hi. Jacob." He almost had to force himself to smile back but he shortly found himself unexpectedly in easy conversation about life in the Caribbean with the young Goth. Despite the unconventional appearance he seemed like a decent kid, intelligent and unexpectedly interested when Jacob mentioned his plans for retirement.

Sam seemed to have a genuine fascination with all things West Indian and asked if Jacob wanted to hear a curious tale about the Caribbean. He was keen to share his story with his captive audience and once he started, the words became a torrent …

"I hate this city in the winter, it's so damned raw," he complained, "But I have an aunt who lived in Barbados before coming here in '66 after she married my uncle. She has told me a lot about life on the islands and I always planned to go there but you know how it is. I see her a lot; we're pretty close really but when my uncle died, she fell on hard times and she spends a lot of time living out on the streets now. During the winter she has a place that she goes to avoid the worst of the cold, I mean, I guess she's around

60 years old now; that's too old to spend winter outside in this town. I do what I can for her but she's very proud; and so stubborn." He paused, far away in some sad thought for a moment before he continued. "What is weird is that she talks about losing Uncle Al as her 'second bereavement' but she's never mentioned the first. She just won't tell me, whatever it was … Don't you think that's a little weird?"

Jacob, intrigued as to where the conversation was going, raised his eyebrows, turned down the corners of his mouth and shrugged his large shoulders, "Go on."

"Hey, don't get me wrong, despite it all she is always cheerful even if she is a little wacky these days. And I really envy her freedom and her refusal to conform. My folks have money; my dad's um, well, let's say he's in business, and my mom; well she enjoys his money. But I tell you man they are so uptight. They don't like people who 'express their individuality' so as you can imagine, looking like this I have to stand on my own. They've pretty much disowned me."

"And your folks don't help your aunt?"

"It's a long story."

"I bet."

Sam changed the subject, "So tell me, do you know anyone in the Caribbean who could use some part-time help? I feel the need for a little sunshine this winter. I could spend the afternoons sitting on the beach, watching the girls and writing stories or poems … That would be awesome."

"Maybe …" Jacob frowned. He liked the kid but for a start he wasn't sure how a Goth would go down in the island culture, and something in his story didn't add up. His curiosity was getting the better of him …

Jacob decided against buying the book; flashy cover, great photos but lacking any real content. As they left the store together, he noticed that the formerly suspicious store owner was now completely distracted by, and unashamedly focussed on, the impressively displayed cleavage of the young woman waiting to pay at the cash register. He was a tall, good-looking man with sandy hair and piercing blue eyes that Jacob imagined had probably lured many a woman back to his lair. Jacob decided he didn't like the man's attitude. *He judges a book by the cover* he thought, smiling as he realised his unintended pun, before shaking his head as recognition dawned that he was being equally judgmental himself.

Jacob and Sam stood together on the bustling sidewalk outside the shop. "You wanna get a cup of coffee?" Jacob offered in his distinctive New York drawl, keen to hear more of the boy's story and with an hour to kill before the music started down by the lake. Sam grinned at the older man and gratefully accepted, "Sure, why not?"

They sunk into the comfortable, worn leather armchairs in Starbucks and looked out onto the bustling street scene as they chatted. Chicago was going about its daily business with people scurrying through their busy lives and no time to enjoy whatever it was they might be achieving. In contrast, an elderly bag lady ambled slowly past the window and glanced in. Jacob noticed her smile, pausing for a moment as though there was a glimmer of recognition. He smiled back through the window; the scarlet flower in her salt and pepper hair, her white teeth somehow out of keeping with her otherwise slightly moth-eaten appearance. In that moment she looked so familiar, but he couldn't place her. She strolled off slowly down Washington towards Michigan Avenue, under the 'L', Chicago's elevated rail track and past the CTA Station, her long powder-blue skirt swinging like a bell, sweeping the sidewalk as she went.

Jacob gazed wistfully after her, not hearing what Sam was saying, trying to place the face that had just looked at him and the walk that somehow seemed so familiar.

"Hey man. Hellooo?" The voice shook him back to reality.

"Sorry Sam, what did you say?"

"That old woman who just looked in who was smiling at me? That was my aunt; the one I'm telling you about."

Jacob was bewildered; "She's … your aunt? But … but she's, well, she's black."

"You wanna hear the rest of the story huh?" Sam smiled.

"I do now," replied Jacob, peering back out of the window to where the old woman had disappeared into the afternoon crowds …

Sam sipped the hot coffee, cradled the cup in his hands and began again.

"Uncle Al was my dad's brother. He worked as a sales executive for the family business and part of his territory included the Caribbean. That is where he met aunt Lilly."

Jacob tilted his head to one side. "Lilly you say?"

"Yeah. Apparently they had both loved fishing."

"Fishing?"

Sam continued with his story … "Al was a really laid-back kinda guy, you know, tolerant, easy-going, a bit of a maverick really. They met on the beach, became friends and spent many weekends together on her small boat; fishing, talking and sooner or later I guess they became lovers. The story goes that their relationship had apparently been very passionate, you know the way Caribbean girls are … Hey, like I need to tell you, right?" He grinned mischievously. Jacob feigned innocence.

"Anyway, the affair became a regular thing and developed into something more. Story is that Uncle Al had never experienced anything like her lust for life, they fished and laughed, he read poetry to her, she cooked him the fish that they caught, and they fell in love. On one of his visits, quite unexpectedly, he married her. Of course, returning to Chicago with a black bride in the 1960s was not quite what a respected Chicago family had planned for, or was prepared to tolerate." Sam paused to take a mouthful of coffee. Jacob, captivated by the tale, urged him to continue.

"My Grandfather immediately disinherited them both,

although he still expected Uncle Al to work for the family firm. He was a successful salesman and money is money, right?"

Jacob sensed the cynicism in Sam's voice. They relaxed back into the comfortable chairs and Sam continued, "Al was in line for a promotion to VP Sales, and he deserved it; he'd worked hard and brought in a ton of business because people liked him.

"But Lilly was an embarrassment?" Jacob asked, more as a statement than a question.

"Exactly. There was no way the family was ever going to accept her so they ostracised both her and Uncle Al. Business had to come first. They had embarrassed the family and they paid the price."

"That must have been one hell of a price," Jacob said thoughtfully," But it must also have been one hell of a love that kept them together."

"Oh for sure, but I always get the feeling it was more so for Al. Don't get me wrong, there is no doubt that Lilly loved him very much, and losing him was just terrible for her. But you remember what I said about the 'second bereavement' thing?

There is more to it, I'm sure, and to be honest, that is why I want to get away to the sun; to write their story."

"You're a writer?"

Sam shrugged, "I think I have a story to tell and I was always pretty good with words; who knows?"

"So what else do you know?"

Sam looked to the ceiling as though recharging with facts before continuing.

"Being newly married of course, Al had very little choice but to keep working; he had to provide for his new wife.

Lilly was a singer, a jazz singer. She had a great voice – still does actually – and she loved to sing. Naturally, she felt guilty about the way Al had been treated so she wanted to do what she could to help. Al objected but she was a strong woman and she soon got work in a jazz club owned by a friend of Al's. My uncle continued to travel until, on one of his trips to Jamaica in 1976, a drunk drove him off the road and he was killed. Aunt Lilly was devastated and wouldn't leave the house for months. She lost her voice and of course, no voice, no job. I'm ashamed to say that the family ignored her and pretty soon she lost everything. That's how she ended up on the streets."

Jacob was intrigued. "How could your family just abandon her in her darkest hour? I don't understand."

"Well, I don't tell people my real last name because of the reactions I get, but if I told you that my family owned some land on Lake Geneva up in Wisconsin, you might understand why I keep my surname quiet."

"Lake Geneva is where the rich and famous of Chicago have their summer houses, right?"

"You got it."

"Jeez, that kind of family wealth huh?"

Sam nodded slowly. "My great grandfather started the

firm in the late 1880s and it' s been making a few bucks ever since."

Jacob remembered reading that you didn't own property on the shores of Lake Geneva with a "few bucks" in the bank; this was where the mega rich owned historic mansions, many of which were maybe used for one or two months of the year. No, a summer home on the lake shore meant you had several million bucks *spare* in the bank.

"I read stuff about families like yours in the newspapers all the time. I can't believe I'm sitting here drinking coffee with the heir to one of the largest fortunes in Chicago."

Sam waved his hand dismissively, "You see, this is precisely why I don't use the name. People get all crazy and stop treating me like ... well, like a normal person. I become part of the legend. Believe me, money makes life easier, but it sure as hell doesn't make you happy. Anyways, like I said, I've been disowned until I 'come to my senses' and become 'normal' again. *'Writer?'* my dad said, *'This family didn't make its money by writing anything except the history in this town.'* I haven't seen much of that money recently but you know what; I don't care, I really am pretty happy just being me; discovering the real me."

Jacob could relate to that, Veronica, his long-departed ex-wife had come from a family with money, and she turned out to be one of the most miserable people he'd ever known. She was terrified to be herself, to live life as she really wanted to. She was always afraid that by doing anything that might upset her somewhat highly-strung father, her inheritance would be lost. And that was a chance she wasn't prepared to take.

What's more, Jacob could now understand why Sam was so keen to share his story. This was a story that would shake the foundations of his family if it ever went to print and the kid was obviously torn over whether to put pen to paper or just let it rest. He was judging Jacob's reaction ...

The two men chatted on through another cup of coffee before saying their farewells. Sam gave Jacob his cell phone number. "Call me if you hear of anything that would keep me in beers down in the islands while I write my story, OK?" He smiled warmly and held out his hand. "It's been a pleasure."

Jacob shook Sam's hand and promised that he would be in touch – and he meant it. He shook his head as he walked towards Grant Park and the festival, but his mind was elsewhere. It had been a fascinating encounter but something else was nagging inside him.

Later that afternoon as he stood under the warm sun in Grant Park listening to a performance of the old Robert Johnson classic *"Sweet Home Chicago"*, Jacob noticed a mocha-skinned young woman with long dark curly hair. She was stylish, pretty and, Jacob couldn't help noticing, had a figure that fitted her jeans to perfection as her hips swayed gently in time with the music. *Mexican, Colombian?* he wondered. He'd never found it easy to tell Latinas apart.

Well I bet she can dance a mean horizontal mambo he thought, grinning mischievously.

Then someone else caught his eye. Standing with her back to him to the left of the pretty girl was Sam's aunt. Was it or not? Jacob furrowed his brow. The name Lilly meant nothing to him but he was certain he knew her. He watched her for a few minutes then, as she turned her head and said something to the girl in the jeans, it struck him; he knew exactly who she was and he felt his pulse quicken. Stepping forward he put his hand lightly on her shoulder. "Martha?" He noticed her scent; not the stench of the streets he might have expected but the much more subtle aroma of flowers.

Startled, the woman turned and looked curiously at Jacob … Suddenly there was a spark of recognition in her dark eyes and a smile broke like dawn across her face. "Jacob? No, it can't be. Jacob Cabral? Oh my God!"

The young woman looked on in amazement as the old woman beside her suddenly threw her arms around the large man's neck and burst into tears.

Lilly, or rather Martha, had been Jacob's first love when he was sixteen. As teenagers they had fished from her father's simple but vividly painted boat on the turquoise Caribbean. It was that experience which had fired his passion for fishing and, ultimately, prompted his retirement dream. But it was not to be. Jacob had grudgingly left the Caribbean when his family decided there were better opportunities for them all in the Big Apple. His protests had fallen on deaf ears and so, heartbroken, he was forced to leave Martha behind. He had always known in his heart that Martha had been the one true love of his life and although he would never admit it, he had secretly hoped that one day they might meet up again. But he never expected it to happen in here in Chicago … and certainly not at the age of sixty-two.

As they sat down to eat later that evening, Jacob couldn't believe he was looking at the same woman he had met earlier. After they had decided to have dinner together, Martha had asked for some time to get herself ready and Jacob had reluctantly agreed, anxious that this was all a dream and if he let her go, he would lose her again. Finally he agreed and had returned to his small hotel to also smarten up as best he could with his limited choice of clothes. But nothing had prepared him for the vision that awaited him in the hotel reception. Martha was no longer the carefree young woman he had loved all those years ago, but she was still beautiful, and she still had *that* smile. With her elegant yet simple outfit and a scarlet hibiscus flower in her hair adding an exotic touch, she looked stunning.

Over a simple dinner of grilled fish, the transformed Martha filled the missing years.

"It broke my heart when you and your family left for New York," she began without any hint of bitterness," and I met Albert while I was still vulnerable. I guess I really married on the rebound from you, but don't get me wrong; I was very lucky. Albert was a good man; a good husband

and despite all the pressure and problems we had from his family, we lived very happily for the ten years we were married. But Jacob, Albert wasn't you, and as much as I loved him, and I did, I had always known that he just wasn't my soulmate. My heart always belonged to someone else … You."

She paused, looking into his eyes, softly stroking his hand and blinking back tears before continuing. "It was Albert who called me Lilly, because I loved flowers so much and he thought that was kinda cute. I used to fill the house to bring a little Caribbean sunshine into the city. But after he was killed I couldn't bear to be in the house anymore. Anyway, I couldn't afford to stay there so I moved into a small apartment above the old jazz club. Then I got a huge surprise. Going through Albert's papers, I found he'd taken out life insurance, to make sure I would be OK if anything happened to him. He knew I'd get nothing from the family. So you see, despite appearances, I'm not destitute at all."

"So how did you end up, you know, on the street?"

Martha smiled, absently twirling her glass of iced water with the right hand.

"I don't live on the streets Jacob. Albert used to give money to help the homeless; that was his thing. I guess he had grown up with such privilege that he hated to see people with nothing. I never expected to have money; I was happy to live a simple life and besides, that family money had brought so much unhappiness I thought it was time to do some good. When the insurance paid out I realised how close I'd become to ending up like those poor people so I decided to help wherever I could. The more time I spent with them, the more fulfilled I felt; it gave me back a reason to live. It was such a contrast to Albert's family who have everything, it made me feel … worthwhile again."

Jacob nodded. That was the Martha he had fallen in love with all those years ago; strong, caring, passionate. "And Sam?" he said, "what's his story?"

"Sam? But how on earth do you know Sam?" A look of puzzlement crossed her face until Jacob explained his bizarrely fortuitous meeting with Sam earlier in the day.

Her eyes lit up and she chuckled, "Ah, Sam. That boy is one of a kind. Albert and I never had children but Sam and I became very close. He loved that I was *different*, and like me, he'd become a bit of an outcast. I guess that's why we get along. He was the only one who kept in touch and made sure I was OK when Albert passed away. We would meet in coffee shops or in the park and just sit and talk. He was always so supportive. But I never even told him about the insurance payout. I didn't want to put him in a difficult position with his folks. How such a nice boy came from such mean parents I will never know," she sighed.

Lilly took a deep breath, "So, that's my story. Now young man, you can tell me what you have been up to for the past forty years …"

They chatted and laughed long into the evening, easy in each other's company, as they had always been. By the time they said goodnight they were flirting like teenagers. Both knew the attraction was still mutual and that they were getting a second chance to love each other; and this time they wouldn't let it pass them by. This time it was forever …

Three months later

It had finally arrived; Jacob's last day at work. The day had dawned bright, a beautiful morning. He'd kissed Martha as she slept serenely and started his last-ever shift early, 4.30 am. Tomorrow he and Martha would be on the plane home and in three days they would be married. Sam had already gone ahead to make the arrangements. After more than forty years, Martha and Jacob were finally going to live out their dream together.

After delivering a few night birds home to their nests, Jacob drove a young couple to JFK to catch the early flight to Denver. At this time of the day it was always worth waiting at the airport for a return fare and sure enough, twenty minutes later, an immaculately dressed businessman climbed in the back of the cab and gave an address in lower Manhattan. Traffic was flowing well at this early hour, the air was clear, the morning sun illuminating the New York architecture. Despite its problems, Jacob was going to miss this city.

The sunlight reflected off the magnificent twin towers of the World Trade Centre, as they stood sentinel-like against the cloudless blue sky, proudly standing guard across the city. This was a good area to be in a cab; there were always decent fares to be had as New York's commercial centre went about its business. After all, *the Suits* as he called them were all on expenses and would often add a decent tip as long as they got that precious receipt; and he was always happy to take a few extra dollars home with him. After dropping off the businessman, Jacob found a taxi stand in a street adjacent to the towers and settled back in his seat to wait for his next customer. He wasn't going to chase fares today he decided; he would let them come to him.

The huge explosion made him duck his head instinctively, then nothing but silence. He looked around then noticed his watch. It was 8.48am; the date showed Sept 11. It only took five seconds before the tons of debris from American Airlines Flight 11, striking the North Tower 100 floors above him, crashed down on Jacob and his yellow cab. He was one of the first to die that day. For Jacob there had been no time for fear, for sadness or regrets, his dream was ended in an instant.

Three agonising months later and despite Sam's unwavering and compassionate support, an inconsolable Martha, dreams shattered and unable to face Christmas alone, became yet another victim of the events of that sunny September morning. She would never be included in the official casualty figures but, at 4.29pm on the afternoon of 23rd December, in the depths of despair and unnoticed by the rest of the world, she threw herself silently beneath the wheels of an Amtrak train as it approached Chicago Union Station. Martha and Jacob were reunited forever.

Epilogue

One year later

The balmy afternoon heat made Sam drowsy as he lolled contentedly aboard his 40ft motor-cruiser *Jacob's Dream*, the fishing line dangling in the warm waters of the Caribbean, a chilled bottle of Red Stripe beer in the shadow cast by his seat. With Jacob and Lilly both gone, and their tragic story written, Sam had decided to live out his own dream now, and spend some of his unforeseen inheritance from Lilly while he still had the chance. He pulled on the cold beer. This was the life they had all expected to be living by now ...

***

Dark Side of the Moon

With ample fuel remaining, our ungainly bug touched down exactly as planned. There was now no sound, save a small vibration from the engine as it cooled in the icy vacuum of space after the descent to the lunar surface. Mission Commander Alan Scott clicked his microphone to 'transmit', *"Stanford, Tranquillity Base here. The Forerunner has landed"*.

Four days, seven hours, forty-five minutes and thirty-two seconds into the mission I took my hands from the controls and looked across the tiny crew compartment of the LEM, the Lunar Excursion Module and gave a thumbs-up sign. "We made it Sir."

Scott smiled, "We sure did buddy; we sure did."

This was the culmination of a long-planned and complex deception, actioned to demonstrate the power wielded by a worldwide elite group of extremely wealthy sociopaths and egomaniacs to undermine the old world order; to prove that they could outperform anything that the world's most powerful governments could achieve. And this was just the first of many such events which they had planned. In just a few short weeks time, the eyes of the world would be glued to TV screens around the globe as, apparently, for the first time ever, a man would set foot on the charcoal grey surface of the moon, utter those eleven scripted words that would be repeated for years to come, and be immortalised forever in the annals of history. That man was Mission Commander Neil Armstrong … At least, that's what the history books would show.

Our crew – mission commander Alan Scott, command module pilot Frank Clark, and myself, LEM pilot Rusty Irwin – all knew that *our* achievement would never be openly acknowledged and we would never be credited. This was something we just had to accept, due to the incredible series of top-secret underhand events which we, the expendable guinea pigs, had been coerced and eventually blackmailed into, and then forced to conceal, even from our families, for the past five years …

After our nerve-wracking descent to the moon's surface, we were told to rest before the next step of our mission. A literal step into history …

Six hours later, the highly secure radio link to Mission Control – located deep underground in Silicon Valley, close to Stanford University in California – crackled into life:

"Okay. Stanford, I'm about ready to go."

"Roger that Alan. Break. Forerunner, this is Stanford. Standing by for your TV link. Over".

"Stanford, this is Alan. Radio check."

"Alan, this is Stanford. Loud and clear. Break. Rusty, this is Stanford. Radio check, and verify TV circuit breaker in."

"Roger, TV circuit breaker's in, and read you five square."

"Roger that Rusty. Break. Alan, we are go for EVA."

"You sure we have to do this?" I asked Alan Scott for what must have been the twentieth time, my radio link with Earth temporarily, but purposely cut.

"What the hell," replied Scott, "let's go make a little history."

A few moments later, Alan Scott stood at the hatch of *Forerunner* where, in a few short weeks, the collective eyes of the world would be focussed on what was happening onboard an identical, angular box called *Eagle sitting* silently, 240,000 miles away from their TV screens. We shook hands and depressurised the cabin. Scott checked his microphone one final time and prepared to deliver some memorable words as he stepped through the hatch and onto the small platform we referred to as 'the porch', outside the LEM. The date was the 1st March 1969.

02:55 GMT on 21st July 1969

The fuzzy black & white image was beamed to a terrestrial

audience of billions who watched as Neil Armstrong slowly descended the ladder to become, what they believed to be, the first human to walk on the surface of the moon, and uttered the immortal phrase, "That's one small step for man; one giant leap for mankind."

The moon landing was, in fact, a relatively minor event in the whole scheme of space exploration. A highly visible PR coup for NASA and the USA for sure, but one which had also acted as an extremely effective smokescreen to a far more important outcome ... the shady, billionaire-funded *Offworld Colonization Plan: the OCP.*

Safely ensconced in the living quarters of the highly-secretive Offworld Colonization Space Station (OCSS), orbiting around two-hundred miles above the Earth, the three of us studiously watched the poor quality TV coverage of the Apollo 11 moon landing. The original mission to launch an experimental space station had officially been abandoned, decreed a failure. But in reality the space station had, in total secrecy, been effectively hijacked by the shadowy *Illuminati.* It was launched, developed and expanded into something far less transitory than originally intended – it had become a futuristic long-term facility which had been used for a number of years as a testing base and transit platform for other more-nefarious activities. It had become the OCSS ...

As we watched the coverage of Armstrong taking that

final long step off the ladder, I commented, "One small step for man? I always said they needed an extra rung on that ladder."

That was the moment when Armstrong suddenly went off-script. Something was wrong; very wrong. Away to his left, the sunlight reflected off something metallic, something that should not have been there. The descent section of another lunar landing craft ...

"Um, Houston, we have a problem – someone has been here before us."

They had the whole goddamned moon to aim for – what were the chances of both craft touching down within one mile of one another? Because of an overload to the limited capacity of the guidance computer onboard *Eagle*, the crew of Apollo 11 had been forced to land their craft manually, and unbelievably it had ended up within spitting distance of where *Forerunner* had landed four months earlier, precisely as planned, and completely unknown to America's official space agency.

This was a potential disaster for NASA. Fortunately the cameras had yet to be panned across the lunar landscape and, due to the very minor delay in the audio signal from the moon, Armstrong's comment had to be immediately and permanently deleted from the radio relay, and from all the official records. His observation would never be heard on the TV or media – but we on the OCSS all heard it. The audio from *Eagle* to Houston suddenly went silent while fifty technicians went into panic mode and the powers-that-be hastily, and in coded words, reminded Armstrong and his crew of their obligations regarding official secrets.

As I write this account I have no idea whether this uncensored memoir will ever be published, somehow I doubt it, but who knows what the future holds? So I'll continue to write it principally for my own benefit. The incredible true account of how I became only the second man to walk on the surface of the moon, four months before Neil Armstrong's historic arrival on the same rock. I can't even imagine the huge disappointment he must have felt for the rest of his life, knowing that despite all the official reports, he had not, in truth, been the *First Man on the Moon*. Nor even the second.

16:50 GMT on 24th July 1969

As the crew of the *Forerunner* and the rest of the world watched the command module of Apollo 11 splashdown safely in the Pacific ocean to complete its successful and historic mission, almost two-hundred miles above the Earth, in the silent vacuum of space, a pre-set electrical relay was triggered and the living quarters aboard the multi-billion dollar space station were suddenly misted with a fine aerosol of lethal gas, and with it, any risk of disclosure by the first men who actually walked upon the surface of the moon was averted forever. Five minutes later, the cabin air was completely vented into space and then fully replenished before the system was automatically closed down. This would allow the next crew to safely dispose of the bodies of the three pioneers into the infinite blackness of space. It had all been meticulously and callously planned long beforehand.

Three weeks later, an explosive charge detonated silently and unseen on the moon and all physical evidence of the *Forerunner* also vanished forever.

Somewhere in California a telephone rang ...

"Lab-rats dealt with. All remaining evidence erased as required."

The recipient of that call may have reacted less smugly if he had known that a handwritten notebook containing an expressly forbidden but highly detailed and hugely revealing account of the whole mission, would resurface many years later, having been surreptitiously retrieved from an icy grave in space by a rare man of principle ...

***

It all Depends on Your Point of View

(Who's to say what infinity means?)

"God, like the universe he created, is infinite. There is nothing greater or more perpetual," Father Patrick preached to his congregation.

Bubbles rising majestically to the surface of the pool absorbed fractured light from the surrounding water, revealing microscopic star-shaped particles of dust within.

As Father Patrick continued his sermon, one bubble broke-surface on the pool and, in that instant, his universe vaporised.

***

Three Spontaneous Dances
A Tale of Love, Lies and Loss

Steve and Laura had married while both still in their very early twenties, both so sure of their love that there seemed no reason to wait any longer, and they had spent more than forty-five happy years together ... until that fateful day.

September 2022

Steve had always been a sceptic; he had never trusted politicians and now, less so than ever. The 'science' they were spouting made no logical sense. He was no Einstein but he did have the ability to think for himself, and to evaluate what he was being told – and none of what they were saying added up.

Laura on the other hand had always been a trusting soul, constantly prepared to see the best in everyone, but Steve still didn't understand why had she had been so trusting of the politicians. Why? Why the hell had the government kept pushing for the damned vaccine when day by day, reports of terrible side-effects appeared in the ever-decreasing trustworthy sources of real news?

They had talked it over and he had tried to convince her

not to be vaccinated before the results of the clinical trials were published, but Laura, like so many others, had been deceived and scared by all the fearmongering. She had been overwhelmed by the constant barrage of propagandistic lies and decided she would have the vaccination, 'just to be on the safe side'. "Don't worry so much love, it must be safe or they wouldn't be able to offer it," she'd said, trusting as always. That was five weeks ago ...

Steve stood alone at the graveside, the rain falling steadily, but he didn't even take notice. All he knew was that his beautiful Laura had gone forever. His tears mixed with the raindrops streaming down his face, his heart ached but his mind was in turmoil, and inside he was filled with unbridled rage. What had initially appeared to be a minor reaction to 'the jab' had suddenly become a fatal blood clot, something rarely seen in a fit, healthy middle-aged woman before the world went crazy. In Steve's mind, the only true 'pandemic' was the disingenuous profusion of lies and misinformation about the supposed safety of the damned mRNA vaccines.

Back inside the home they had shared happily for so many years; the home in which they had raised their family, Steve removed his muddy boots and saturated coat, before drying his hair on a small hand towel, and then poured himself a large glass of Scotch. He sat down, sipped the whisky and tried to think of some way to numb the ever-present pain of losing Laura, but of course, that was impossible.

His mind drifted back almost fifty years, and he clearly remembered the night that Laura had first come to contact with the duplicitous Mark Lombard, the youth whose lewd advances she had once rejected; the former womanising party-goer who had somehow risen to become the official 'Pandemic Spokesman'. The disingenuous and smug minister who had sold out any principles he may once have possessed to become the government's mouthpiece. For the past year or more he had been forcing the unproven and, as it turned out, largely ineffective experimental 'vaccine' onto the British population. Mark Lombard, who had grown to become the politician who spent hour after hour on TV coercing the public into accepting a drug. A hastily produced and inadequately tested drug which had ultimately taken the life of Steve's beautiful wife – and that, as far as Steve was concerned, made Lombard nothing more that a contemptible, uncaring drug dealer.

Steve put his head in his hands and sobbed uncontrollably. This was a nightmare – Except it wasn't.

With the desolation he felt growing in his now-barren heart, nothing seemed to matter anymore. Dejected, he closed his eyes and slowly returned to happier times, and the unlikely train of events in which he and Laura had first fallen for each other. Serendipity had certainly been at work way back then ...

July 1975
If he'd never bought that motorbike, none of this would have happened ...

As a teenager, Steve had bought his first motorcycle – a sporty little 125cc Yamaha – so that he could get to work each day. On the day it was delivered, he perched onboard it excitedly for the first time, but his audience at home was less impressed. To say that his parents were unhappy about his choice of transport, as many are in the same situation, would be an understatement, but in reality, they knew that he couldn't afford to run a car and he needed transport to get to his new job as an apprentice aircraft engineer, situated at a small airport fifteen miles from his home. But as he would come to realise, a motorbike didn't need to be *just transport*. As it is said, *'four wheels move the body; two wheels move the soul'*, and as he would discover, the little bike gave Steve a freedom he'd never experienced before, and he welcomed that opportunity with open arms.

When a friend had introduced him to a group of mates who also rode bikes, for the first time in his life, Steve felt part of something special – the motorcycle fraternity that he would come to know so well. They may have looked a motley crew but were, in reality, a group of decent, if somewhat hirsute lads, who loved the freedom and individuality that a motorbike afforded them. Steve had never experienced such close friendships and camaraderie before. As his self-confidence grew he started meeting up regularly with the lads in pubs, occasionally at parties, and very infrequently, even the occasional Glam-rock disco, all things he had never enjoyed in the past – and he still wasn't convinced about the discos. Neither had he been very self-assured with girls. Being fairly naive in that arena, he was often out of his comfort zone in their company. That was until one evening in the Eagle Tavern, a traditional and characterful pub in a small Kentish town not far from Folkestone. The *Eagle* was set back from the main road with a large car park to the rear. Inside it featured several original etched and cut glass windows and mirrors so popular in pubs in years gone by. It was a bit of a time warp really with a dartboard and bar-billiards table, which only added to its appeal and as it was easily accessible for most of the lads, they had made it their default venue for their evenings out.

One of the group, Jim, had brought his new girlfriend, Laura along with him. They had arrived on foot as Laura's parents, not exactly thrilled with their daughter's choice, wouldn't dream of letting her get on a motorbike with, as they put it, "That long-haired, scruffy bugger," and of course everyone ribbed Jim about being 'under the thumb'. Inevitably, after this challenge to his manliness and his first pint of bitter, Jim invited a few of the others to a game of darts, which he saw as a way to prove his worth, and the others all readily accepted.

Steve found himself sitting with Laura, who was unimpressed with the macho posturing, and Rob: tall, gangly with a mop of curly dark hair, and a large aquiline nose. Rob was easily-bored with anything other than drinking his pint and talking ad-nauseam about bikes. Unsurprisingly, when the conversation regarding the benefits of Ducati's *desmodromic* valve gear or the idiosyncrasies of Norton's *isolastic* engine mounts didn't progress very far with Steve and Laura, Rob moved off to find someone more mechanically inclined, leaving Steve and Laura alone at the table.

Laura was the same age as Steve and although perhaps slightly tomboyish, she was sophisticated and exquisitely attractive; far more than just a pretty face. She was slim with shortish blonde hair, centrally parted and swept back at the sides, and had the most inviting smile. Initially, Steve felt a little awkward. Although he found her very enticing, with his relative inexperience with girls, he wasn't confident to start the conversation, but Laura sensed his nervousness and soon put him at ease, inviting him to tell her about himself and in turn, chatting easily about her love of painting and drawing

"So tell me about you, apart from the bikes I mean," she asked.

"Not much to tell really," he replied humbly, "I'm happy, healthy and not very exciting, but that's improving since I met this bunch of reprobates. They tend to bring me out of my shell, whether I like it or not."

"I know what you mean. But from what I see, they're a pretty good bunch."

"They are, and all smarter than you might think. At first glance you might underestimate that."

"Never judge a book by the cover eh?" she said.

"Exactly." He shuffled on the uncomfortable pub chair and relaxed a little in her company. "So what about you?" he asked, "I don't really see you as a biker chick so what's your story?"

Her answer surprised him. "Art is my thing actually. And I've never been on a bike in my life, but I could probably draw one." She smiled again.

"Okay, that's unexpected. The art thing I mean."

"Well it's only a hobby at the moment, I enjoy sketching and dabble in oil painting occasionally, but I'm hoping to go to uni and study it properly one day."

"Good for you, live your dream eh? Any favourite artists?"

"A couple, but art is very subjective. It's difficult to describe what makes art 'good'. Are you interested in art then?"

"Not with any knowledge, I just know what I like."

"Okay, well that's equally unexpected. I've haven't met many art-loving bikers before."

"Ha ha. Actually I can do better than that ... I like classical music too."

"Classical? Seriously? I'd have thought you were more of a rock fan."

"Well I like rock too: you know, Pink Floyd, Led Zep, Deep Purple. Actually, do you know Roger Dean, the artist who does the album covers for Yes?"

"Of course; I love Roger Dean's work. He's an amazing artist."

She also admitted that she loved the Prog-rock music of *Yes*. Steve however thought it was horribly discordant. He just liked the incredible fantasy landscapes on their album covers. But with the ice now broken, Steve and Laura chatted easily.

Steve had earlier said that he didn't know much about art, but then, taking Laura completely by surprise, he mentioned a painting called *Metamorphosis of Narcissus* by Salvador Dali, and a Van Gogh painting, 'the one with the cypress tree and the moon' – he didn't know its name but thought it was beautifully atmospheric. She was very familiar with them both and *Metamorphosis* was actually one of her own personal favourites.

"Very discerning choices," she agreed. "The one with the tree and the moon is actually called *Road with Cypress and Star,* with a stunning, swirling Van Gough sky," she told him with no hint of egotism.

He was very impressed, but so was she. This was not the conversation she had expected from a quietly-spoken biker. Never judge a book etc., she thought ... again.

Discovering this unanticipated mutual interest, they were soon talking comfortably together, but the conversation was cut short when the noise from the darts game rose to a crescendo as Richard, a good-humoured, slightly dishevelled artist who, despite being a victim of the Thalidomide scandal which had left him with a distorted right leg and malformed hands, still threw the winning arrow, and Jim graciously accepted defeat. The happy, laughing friends descended on the table where Laura and Steve were sitting and that had brought an end to their first conversation.

"More drinks anyone?" asked Richard as he savoured his victory.

Eventually the band of friends bade each other goodnight, donned their helmets and leather jackets and mounting their eclectic mix of machines, roared off up the high street, all waving happily to the pedestrian couple, as Jim walked Laura home. Steve couldn't help but feel a pang of envy as he rode past them with a wave of his hand. *Lucky sod,* he thought, *I wouldn't mind kissing her goodnight myself.*

Three minutes later, Dave, another friend of the group who had been struggling to get his Dad's fickle, twenty-year-old moped – the inappropriately named *NSU Quickly*

– to fire-up, finally set off from the pub. Hunched over the handlebars and trailing a large blue nebula of two-stroke smoke, he was less-than-pleased to be overtaken by a dog, running along the footpath beside him. This occurred despite the fact that Dave was also pedalling like mad to assist the asthmatic engine; desperately trying to coax the antiquated velocipede into achieving its terminal velocity of 25mph. About fifteen seconds later, a little further up the road, he too waved cheerfully at the sauntering couple as they were left engulfed by his blue miasma.

A few weeks later, much to the relief of Laura's parents, Jim and Laura went their separate ways, but they still remained amiable and Laura became a regular part of the group of friends whenever they met-up at the local pubs, and she always had a smile for Steve. He was certainly attracted to her and she was clearly still single, but he still felt terribly shy talking to her, especially with all his mates around him. So despite the attraction, they remained little more than casual acquaintances. But that was about to change ...

The turning point came on a warm Saturday evening several weeks later at a party. These events usually happened at the house of whoever's parents were away for the weekend, which was just as well considering the volume of the music, the abundance of alcohol and the fug of *wacky baccy* that pervaded the living room. Steve arrived at the party with Richard, Rob and Gary, a friend who worked for the Post Office and whose extraordinary and unique approach to dancing had earned him the nickname *The Schizophrenic Postman*. They all turned up in Richard's latest pride and joy, an ancient Austin A35, having just passed his driving test a few weeks earlier; the first of the group to do so in a car.

In time-honoured fashion, carrier bags full of beers were deposited in the kitchen and Steve, with a can of Double Diamond in hand, wandered into the living room. Sitting on the sofa was Laura, clearly trying to repel the unwanted advances of a guy that Steve recognised as Mark, a lad he'd been introduced to once before and had taken an instant dislike to. Mark was slightly older than Steve, irritatingly good-looking but totally self-obsessed and egotistic. Steve was annoyed to see him unsubtly trying his luck with Laura who, despite Mark's efforts, appeared to be well in control of the situation, and of his wandering hands. Unexpectedly irritated by the scene but thinking it would be inappropriate to interfere, after all, he hardly knew her, he turned around and, somewhat grumpily, made his way back to the kitchen where he made small talk with a couple of the other party-goers. About ten minutes later, Laura appeared looking a little flustered and proceeded to pour herself a large glass of white wine. As she turned to leave the kitchen she noticed Steve, smiled shyly and said, "Hello there." There was little to suggest any desire to get into a deeper conversation at that point.

The party was in full swing and had by now overflowed the house into the back garden. The music was loud and most of the biker crowd were dancing wildly – none quite as wildly as Gary – to *Wishing Well* by Free as Steve, his inhibitions slowly fading after a couple of drinks, made his way through the living room with the intention of perhaps joining in the merriment happening in the garden. He was relieved to see that having failed to make any impact in Laura's affections, Mark had moved on to another potential conquest and was engrossed in an intimate embrace in the corner of the room. Laura was now sitting alone, happily people-watching from the sofa, and in a totally out-of-character moment, Steve decided it was now or never.

"Hello again," he said, "Are you enjoying the party?"

"Oh, hi. I'm not really much of a party girl to be honest but it's okay. How about you?"

"Yeah, it's okay, but I wouldn't say I was the life and soul either. In fact I very nearly gave it a miss."

"Why's that? What's up?"

"Oh, nothing in particular, just feeling a bit jaded. Busy week, you know."

"It's Steve, right?"

"You remembered."

"Of course. We share a love of art if I remember correctly, and not many in our little crowd of bike fanatics have anything interesting to say about the finer things in life." She smiled, "Please, have a seat," she indicated to the cushion beside her.

"No, I'm fine thanks, really." His insecurity was kicking in again.

"Come on," she insisted, "sit beside me so we can talk again. I've been hoping that I would see you again."

Steve felt flattered. "Really? Well, OK, if you're sure?"

She smiled and repeated softly, "Please, sit."

Steve sat ...

What he couldn't possibly have known at the time was that Laura had sensed his interest in her when they had first chatted in the pub a few weeks' earlier, and had also found herself very attracted to him with his gentle humility and eclectic tastes. But she also thought she'd detected an underlying strength, a competitive streak perhaps that he was unable to completely suppress. *He is deeper than he first appears*, she thought. She found Steve's quiet and less-pushy demeanour to be a breath of fresh air amongst all the usual emerging testosterone in most lads her age; and definitely so much more appealing than Mark Lombard's earlier suggestive and lewd chat-up lines. In fact, her burgeoning feelings for Steve had made it easy for her to reject that lothario Mark and his blatant attempt to seduce her. Those same feelings had also been a fundamental part of the break-up with Jim who was a decent-enough guy but it had soon become apparent that there was no real spark between them; unlike the immediate chemistry she'd experienced with Steve. However, she could clearly see that despite her own natural reserve, if she didn't make the first move here, this potential relationship may never get off the ground.

Steve smiled at her, noticing how blue her eyes looked, even in the dark, smoky room, and he relaxed. As with their previous encounter, her amiable nature seemed to put him at his ease.

"I've heard it said that we all have a bohemian streak in us somewhere," he said, clumsily trying to make conversation. "Actually, I really envy you," he continued, "I'd love to be able to paint or draw but I have one small drawback ... No talent. My only potential contribution to the arts world is with words. I used to write stories and poems but I haven't even done that for ages, although I could easily be inspired by those beautiful blue eyes of yours."

Laura laughed, "Why thank you kind sir. You're a smooth-talker aren't you?" and without thinking, she leaned across and kissed him softly on the lips. She had surprised herself with the uncharacteristic boldness of her approach.

Steve however was completely stunned. This fortuitous turn of events stirred in him a powerful emotion, the like of which he had never-before encountered, and it provided him the unforeseen confidence to respond in kind. He gazed deep into her enticing blue eyes. Despite the darkness of the room, they sparkled invitingly. She's not just attractive, he thought, she's actually rather beautiful, and at that moment, with his courage at an all-time high, he pushed a stray lock of hair back from her face, placed his hand behind her head and gently pulled her towards him. Their lips met again. Her response was exquisite and as they kissed, she ran her fingers through his unkempt locks.

"I love your hair," she said gently, "It's so curly." It was said with a soft west-country burr.

"I never noticed that you had an accent before," he said, "Where is that from?"

"I was born in Somerset, but I thought I'd lost the accent long ago," she explained.

"Nope, afraid not," he replied, smiling at her once more, "but it's very endearing."

"You're too kind."

Before he had a chance to reply, Richard appeared in front of them. "You two look as though you are getting to know each other," he said, grinning in that irritatingly knowing way that people do.

"We were, before you arrived," replied Steve good-naturedly but blushing slightly. He hadn't realised they'd had an audience.

"Well, I'm sorry about that but I need to steal this pretty lady for a dance," said Richard, and with that he whisked Laura to her feet and whirled her around the floor. *Pretty good mover for a bloke with wonky legs,* thought Steve as he watched them laughing together. He'd already been told that Laura and Richard had been friends for several years with their mutual interest in art, but he still felt a small pang of jealousy. He smiled at them and wandered out into the garden to watch the unfolding mayhem of Gary, the Schizophrenic Postman, and Rob frantically doing their best Mick Jagger impersonations to *Brown Sugar* – lips puckered, hips gyrating and beer cans in hand – and both completely out of synch with the music.

Presently, Steve returned to the darkened living-room and was delighted when Laura, back on her sofa after tripping the light fantastic with Richard, beckoned him to sit with her again.

"Feeling any better now?"

"Yes, much better thanks. Nothing cheers you up like watching Gary do his best Mick Jagger," he replied with a laugh. "How was your less-manic boogie with the Sugar Plum Fairy?"

"Rich is actually a pretty good dancer considering his obvious challenges,"

"From what I see, he's not one to let that hold him back from anything."

"Very true, and I admire that. So, anyway," she continued, completely changing the subject, "you came back to sit with me. Any particular reason?"

"Hmm, let me think ..." He drew her tenderly towards him, and continuing their own passionate tango, they kissed again, but at length, and more enthusiastically this time. "Oh yes," he smiled, "now I remember."

Conscious of their surroundings and in an attempt to cool their ardour for a while, they resumed their verbal voyage of discovery and by now, unsurprisingly, they had become relaxed in each-other's company. They discovered that they actually shared a number of interests, and that both were curious and inquisitive souls.

Steve certainly hadn't expected this delightful encounter, but he was really uplifted that the rather gorgeous and, as he discovered, very intelligent Laura wanted to spend her time with him.

Sometime later – neither had any idea how much later – Laura's friend Sally arrived at the sofa.

"Sorry to interrupt but we really need to leave now Laura. Tom and Tina have offered to take us home. I don't know about you but I hadn't made any other plans to get home so, shall we?"

Reluctantly, Laura stood up and looked at Steve. "Thanks for making it such a lovely evening," she said softly, "I really enjoyed it. Maybe we could do this again sometime?"

"I'd love to," he replied; a little too eagerly he thought. "I really loved your company, and you're not a bad kisser either."

"You're not so bad yourself," she smiled back.

Steve grinned, held her close and kissed her one last time. "Just checking!"

"Come on lovebirds," Sally scolded cheerfully, "Time to go; our carriage awaits."

Steve whispered softly "Bye Laura. See you soon I hope," and with that she was gone ...

Thirty seconds later a sudden feeling of disquiet engulfed

him... IDIOT! Lost in the moment, he hadn't asked where she lived or got her phone number. What a fool. But now fate would play its part.

A somewhat dejected hour and a few beers later, Steve also prepared to leave the party and was just climbing into the back seat of the old A35 as a very drunk Jim came stumbling over and shouted to him, "31 Drake's Avenue."

"What?"

"31 Drake's Avenue, that's where she lives."

"Who?"

"Laura of course. We're pissed, not blind; we all saw you two together. Go for it, she obviously likes you," Jim yelled, before falling headlong into a bush at the side of the driveway.

"Cheers mate," Steve called back as the ancient Austin, with its inebriated occupants, groaned out of the driveway.

Despite his own level of intoxication, Steve managed to ascertain from Richard and, surprisingly, even to remember, Laura's surname and exactly where she lived. With his bravado buoyed by the drink and emboldened by the confidence-boosting memory of that first kiss, he vowed he would call on her, and soon. For the first time in his life he had found a girl who had awakened feelings in him that he didn't even know existed.

He had a really good feeling about this ...

Unwelcome Visitors

Scott needed to write, and his deadline was looming. It really had to be written but today there was so much going through his head that the words refused to come. His divorce papers had arrived today and he felt powerless to do anything about it. Amy had been his life and when, for no apparent reason, she had coolly announced that she wanted to end their five-year marriage, his plans for the future, like his wife, had disappeared overnight. That was six weeks ago. He hadn't heard a word from her since, until today ... What did she mean by *'unreasonable behaviour'?*

Usually a walk, or ten minutes reading the newspaper unlocked his writer's block but today, everything distracted him from the task in hand. He looked at the photo of his soon to be ex-wife in the frame beside his computer screen. The day Amy had accepted his marriage proposal, his life had seemed replete. He had never really expected to be married to the most beautiful and elegant woman he had ever laid eyes on and yet, through their work and shared frustrations with the political system, they had become close and then fallen for each other completely. What he had never understood was why she hadn't published the

9/11 theory they had been working on together. But if she wouldn't write it, he would. It was still a great story.

He began to type ... '*Had the US government been 'involved' with the terror attacks on the twin towers and the Pentagon in order to justify going to war with their old adversary, Saddam? This was the question being asked by several respected US commentators who, almost two years after the horror of 9/11 and with the subsequent changes in world events, were now looking with a more critical eye into the events of that bright September morning which had touched the world so profoundly.*'

He had re-written the paragraph several times but it was no good, the words just wouldn't flow. He rubbed his eyes, reached for a CD and slipped it into the player. The velvet voice of the old Cuban club singer Ibrahim Ferrer wafted through the room and within a few moments Scott was transported to the crumbling colonial splendour of Havana, the city he had fallen in love with several years earlier when he and Amy had visited. He well-remembered how her cool elegance had been a great hit with the local Lotharios.

He also remembered that way back in 1962, Cuba had also been the target for the all-powerful but often-paranoid United States when the US Joint Chiefs of Staff had submitted their plan for 'Operation Northwoods'. This proposed staging several false flag 'terrorist' attacks both within the US and on American interests abroad, cleverly engineering the perception of the events so the blame would fall squarely on Cuba. This was to be used as a pretext for the US to invade Cuba, overthrow the Russian-backed Castro and finally remove the threat from the irritating little Communist outpost lying just 90 miles off the southern coast of the United States. Kennedy hadn't been a stupid man; he had ruled against the action, but President George W. Bush's judgement had already been called into question several times. He was another matter altogether. But if the US had the ability to stage such complex operations back in 1962, they could certainly do the same but with much greater global impact in the highly technological world of 2001. Reading through Amy's research documents, it became clear to Scott that some of her theories about the 9/11 attacks could well be closer to the truth than he had first thought and the more he read, it became blindingly obvious that in fact, she had finally uncovered some irrefutable evidence. Now the direction of the story was forming easily in his mind and, under the watchful eye of the beautiful Amy, his fingers typed the first words into his computer, *'Finally, conclusive proof that the US government was both complicit in the staging of, and the cover-up required to hide the real truth of the 9/11 terror attacks'*

In the bowels of a remote facility near Silicon Valley, a monitoring programme raised an electronic red-flag, and an alert was issued ...

Two and a half thousand miles away, Scott's estranged

wife was locked in a filthy cell in a secret CIA detention centre on the outskirts of Havana, looking far from beautiful, and wishing she had never laid eyes on Paulo. Her Latino lover was in fact a US government agent whose fawning fascination with her was far from romantic. He was more intent on preventing her potentially ruinous and surprisingly accurate theory from ever reaching the press. She had tried arguing her right to publish, but a quick beating had soon 're-educated' her. How had they known about her story? Tears welled in her eyes until she heard the key turn in the lock and Paolo and two associates entered the gloomy room. Oh God, what now?

As he finished reading through the completed first draft, the abrupt ring of the doorbell made Chris jump. He looked at the clock. Who could possibly be calling on him at 2.30 am?

***

Buckle up and Fly Right

He waited for his instructor to finish discussing the windspeed with a colleague and climb into the rear seat of the glider. During the long delay before the launch, he'd sat quietly contemplating the flight ahead, his seatbelts slackened to make himself more comfortable in the confines of the snug, open-topped cockpit of the ancient wood and canvas flying machine.

Ten minutes later, one thousand feet up over the English countryside, his instructor put the glider into a stall. As always, the nose came up and the forward motion all but stopped ... Silence for a second ... That beautiful moment as you hung in space before the machine fell, nose first from the sky, and his challenge was to recover from the dive before becoming part of the landscape.

But this time it was different. In one heart-stopping moment he felt himself falling forwards ... falling over the front of the glider as it dived towards the ground. He watched his arm shoot forward in a valiant attempt to brace himself against the instrument panel, and the inevitable death that was surely merely seconds away ...

Her mouth was bleeding. Why did he hit her? Why? He was so much bigger than her ... he didn't have to hit her. Tears welled in her eyes but she wouldn't let him see that he'd hurt her − Why? They had been making love not twenty minutes earlier but now; now she hated him, the jerk. This wasn't what she wanted. What happened to all the nice guys who didn't feel threatened by an intelligent woman? They were a myth, she decided ... a fanciful idea in a young woman's romantic dream. If she was going to survive in this world she was going to have to be tougher.

He sat down quietly, immediately pulling the seat belt around his lap and pushed the two ends of the buckle together until they snapped into place with a dull metallic clunk. It was just a habit really, to immediately secure his seatbelt every time he took his seat. Pure superstition, even after 30 years. He didn't really believe it would make a blind bit of difference if the gleaming aluminium tube was going to plough into the ground anyway. It was just one of those irrational actions, just to ensure he didn't get distracted and forget to buckle up before the Virgin Atlantic Boeing 747 hurtled down almost three miles of tarmac that constitutes runway 27-R of London's Heathrow Airport at 160 knots. Now, safely strapped in, he relaxed and picked up the in-flight magazine from the seat pocket in front of him. A bead of sweat formed on his forehead despite the coolness of the air-conditioned cabin ...

He was on his way to meet her for the first time. They had been speaking on and off for about six months. What had started as a business relationship had developed into friendship and eventually they had decided to meet up and spend a week together. Nervous? Of course. They were both old enough to know better, but this was exciting, and life could have little-enough excitement if you didn't go and look for it.

She had thought he was crazy, getting on a plane and flying 4,000 miles to meet someone he'd never seen ... He thought she was crazy inviting a man she didn't really know to spend a week at her home. Maybe they were both crazy, but neither was really worried. To each of them this felt right – very right.

Four General Electric turbofan engines, each with almost 58,000 lbs of thrust, blasted tons of hydrocarbons into the atmosphere every hour, leaving in their wake, transient white contrails, painted across the heavenly canvas that perhaps God, in one of those creative moments of his, had considerately pre-stained a deep blue in perfect contrast. An ephemeral work of art that someone on the ground 32,000 feet below would look up and see, and wonder where the lucky artists above then, with their high-tech paintbrush, were going on this cold November day.

She glanced out of her kitchen window as, a thousand feet overhead, a sparkling silver American Airlines Boeing 767 descended gently toward the runway of the nearby airport, something that happened every two or three minutes of the day. How soon before his aircraft arrived? She looked at her watch ... Four more hours yet. Was everything ready? What was she doing? She didn't know this man. Would he be as nice when she met him as he'd seemed on the phone? And what if he wasn't? As long as he didn't hit her. She winced as the memories of her former lover flooded back ... What was she doing?

"Tea or coffee sir?" His mind drifted back to the present as he looked at her quizzically and pulled the headphones from his ears. "Tea, coffee?" she enquired again.

"Tea please", he said pleasantly, holding up the flimsy plastic cup, and thanked her. He wasn't really watching the film but having the headphones on meant that none of his fellow-passengers disturbed him. No inane banter from someone who just happened to occupy the seat next to him and who had the unsolicited urge to share their life story with anyone who would listen. He certainly didn't want to share his current situation with anyone. They probably wouldn't have believed him anyway ... he barely believed it himself. For a moment his thoughts were elsewhere; far behind him across the sea. His divorce had been a long, painful and hateful business but now he was ready to move on. The memories of the furious rows had faded and he was sure he was ready to trust again. His mind came back across the Atlantic Ocean that slipped almost imperceptibly past the belly of the huge jet as it thundered across the sea at Mach 0.8

Yes, it was time to move on.

She always considered herself to be 'one of the boys'. Many of her friends were male and she loved going hiking with them. They all knew she wasn't interested in anything more so they didn't even try. Having a Latin-American temperament, she could be pretty formidable despite her petite stature. Yes, she was one tough woman – on the surface at least. But neatly folded and tucked away in the darkest recess of her heart was a desire she refused to face; a longing to be loved, really loved for who she was and not just how she looked – and she looked pretty good for a thirty-four-year-old. It wasn't going to happen though; she wouldn't let it happen, there was always too much pain involved. But she did hope that he'd be cute … He sounded really cute.

He unclipped the seatbelt and stood up, reaching into the overhead locker to get his bag. He was probably bringing far too much with him, but aware that there was every possibility of ending up staying in a hotel, better safe than sorry. His fingers drummed impatiently on the seat-back in front of him.

The little silver Honda Civic pulled into the airport parking space at the time his flight was due to land. Knowing it would take at least 30 minutes to get through immigration, baggage reclaim and Customs, she had called ahead and checked that the flight was on time, and now she felt that twinge of expectation tighten in her stomach. Would they recognise each other from their descriptions? She had been honest, but had he? Her leg bounced up and down nervously as she sat waiting.

Thirty more minutes...

The Start of the Affair

"You know this is wrong, don't you?" Andy whispered as he nuzzled into her neck, "I mean, you are still married, even if you don't want to be."

"Mmm, I know," Lisa replied, still slightly breathless and damp with sweat from their exertions of the past forty minutes, "but I don't make a habit of this and I haven't felt this way for so long."

"But ... it's still wrong." His moral uncertainty was re-emerging, having been temporarily discarded in the heat of their passion; and now he felt guilty. Yes, she was beautiful; yes, her husband had mistreated her, both physically and mentally, but even considering all that, she was still somebody else's wife; that much was fact. This first anxious coupling had been amazingly fulfilling for them both, but deep down they both knew it really shouldn't have happened. At least, not yet.

Andy swung his legs out of the bed and sat on the edge of the mattress, his mind a tangle of rights and wrongs. He looked over his shoulder; she smiled at him – that big wonderful smile that made him melt every time – her long, brunette mane draped across the pillow before she sat up, shuffled closer, and wrapped her arms around him, unsubtly demonstrating that further temptation was right behind him. How could any red-blooded man be damned for surrendering to her charms?

They had been brought together by a mutual colleague, Julie, who, one quiet Thursday afternoon after everyone else had left the office, had been chatting to Andy about life in general, and he had voiced his general discomfort when it came to starting a new relationship. After everything he had been through recently, his confidence was at an all-time low, but in passing, he had, rather imprudently perhaps, mentioned Lisa's downcast look. Julie, wise beyond her twenty-five years, immediately sensed a deeper interest, and had mischievously decided to play Cupid. Aware of the state of Lisa's marriage she had, somewhat indelicately, mentioned to Lisa that Andy thought she was a lovely-looking woman but always had an aura of sadness about her. Because of that unsolicited intervention, Andy now sat on the edge of his bed which was occupied by the most adorable woman he'd known for many years. This hopeful but forlorn, gorgeous woman whose handsome husband, a successful and wealthy stockbroker, had enjoyed parading as a trophy wife to his mates but, it transpired, had no idea of what really made his beautiful wife happy ... Together, Andy and Lisa had just passionately, but tenderly, resolved that issue.

When Julie had voiced Andy's comments to her, Lisa had been flattered, and genuinely surprised that anyone had even noticed her emotional state rather than just her looks. She knew that she still had the visual appeal that men liked; she was tall, long-legged with long dark hair and, due to not having been subjected to the rigours of childbirth, still possessed the kind of figure that turned heads. But the simple fact that Andy had noticed her underlying wistfulness, something she always tried, but clearly failed, to disguise, made her deliberately take a few minutes to interact with him the next time he'd walked past her desk. That simple interaction was the beginning of something that neither had expected, but both longed for; the attention of someone who really cared, and a relationship which offered something more than just a physical attraction.

Andy always hoped he would meet someone with whom he could slowly repair the psychological damage caused by his acrimonious divorce, but of all people, he had never expected it would be Lisa who showed any interest in him. He was just an unremarkable divorced bloke with a mortgage he couldn't afford, whereas she was apparently happily-married, gorgeous, and with a smile to die for – on the rare occasions she chose to show it – but it was those pretty blue eyes with their tinge of melancholy that both captivated and intrigued him. Why should someone with her virtues ever need to look so downcast? After a few weeks, that had all become clear; Lisa needed to rediscover herself, and to be loved again. Really loved, and appreciated.

Foregoing the temptation of another passionate dalliance that was clearly on offer, Andy's self-control finally kicked in again. It was time for them both to go back to the office, and preferably not exhibiting the tell-tale aura brought about by their lunchtime of passion, something which Lisa would later refer to as her 'freshly ravaged look'. As he attempted to rise from the bed he turned to kiss his sad-eyed lover on the nose, before unwinding her arms from around his waist, scolding her playfully, and heading for a quick restorative cold shower. Lisa pouted at him, stuck out half an inch of tongue and stretched noisily. He smiled at her. They had opened Pandora's Box and had no idea what the future held, but they both knew their lives were about to change forever …

***

Knock Knock Knocking on Heaven's Door

"What the bloody hell is that thing doing there?" Jimmy complained as he made his usual loud arrival into the transport office after he had reversed his van past the large caravan which had appeared in the yard since he was last there.

"Don't worry, it's only temporary. Doing someone a favour that's all," said Graham, Jimmy's boss with a wry smile, "I think you'll approve."

A world class stitch-up was just about to be enacted.

Jimmy was known to frequent ladies of the night whilst away for a week or two, working as a long-distance truck driver. He was a single man so nobody seemed to mind as long as he didn't try to claim back the cost of his dalliances on his expenses. But he did like to brag about his conquests.

The truth was that the caravan belonged to a telecoms engineer who needed to be on-site for a week to carry out site maintenance on and around a telephone mast located just behind the warehouse. Graham had allowed the engineer to leave his caravan in the secure yard for a few days while he worked on the mast – as long as he had a sense of humour.

What Jimmy was going to be told on this Friday afternoon was something completely different, and after a long tiring ten-day trip, he was certainly susceptible to the deception that was about to unfold.

"So what's with the caravan then?" Jimmy grumbled.

"I told you, I just thought I'd do someone a favour," replied Graham.

"Go on ..."

"Well, how can I put this delicately? It belongs to a tart who's been evicted from where she was parked up before."

Jimmy's eyes widened. "You *are* joking?"

"No, I'm serious. I said she could park up here for a week or so."

"No way!"

"It's true Jim," confirmed Mike, the quiet and serious office manager, "and she's quite a looker too."

"Bloody hell!"

"But it's no good you getting any idea about a quickie before you go home, she's already *busy*."

Jimmy was still sceptical, but knowing Graham as he did, this was just the kind of thing he would do ... But Jimmy's suspicions were finally allayed when Peter, the telecoms engineer – amused when Graham had told him about the ruse – showed up at the office door and declared, "Hello lads. I see the entertainment's arrived then." As Peter was not one of Jimmy's colleagues and unlikely to be involved in any pranks, Jimmy was now convinced ... and keen to make the most of this unexpected opportunity.

"Anyway Jim," Graham scolded cunningly, "bugger off and get unloaded or you'll be here all night,"

"Okay, okay. Here's your paperwork from my run. Put the kettle on and I'll be back shortly." Jimmy thrust a wad of shipping documents into Mike's hand and trudged off to unload his van; but not before knocking on the door of the caravan just to check whether his *Miss Whiplash* was in fact, 'otherwise engaged'.

Three other drivers and the rest of the office team waited until he was well out of earshot before erupting into gales of laughter. Knowing Jimmy as they all did, it came as no surprise to any of them that he had completely and utterly fallen for the prank.

Jimmy returned about ten minutes later, completely flustered and vociferous, "Have you seen that? The bloody caravan's actually rocking! She must be one hell of a performer."

The other lads all went to the door of the office and, sure enough, there was definitely movement from within the caravan. "Blimey, he's right."

What they all knew, but Jimmy didn't, was that Peter

had gone into the caravan while Jimmy was unloading his van, watched through the net curtains for Jimmy's return and then started moving his weight from one leg to the other and moaning noisily.

"I've got to have some of that." Jimmy announced lustfully.

"You just missed out when you went to unload," said Mike helpfully, "the previous bloke left and this fella was straight in there."

"Bollocks, bloody typical," Jimmy complained. "Well maybe by the time I've had my tea he'll be finished."

"Here you go mate. Build your strength up for the task ahead," said Mike as he offered a biscuit to go with Jimmy's mug of steaming tea. It was not only the tea that was steaming. Jimmy positioned himself so that he could keep an eye on the caravan through the open door of the office. He didn't want to miss his chance again.

After more rocking and moaning, the door of the caravan finally opened and Peter the telephone man emerged looking suitably knackered. Jimmy was on his feet like a shot and ready for his own performance. "Bloody hell, that bloke looks half-dead. Wish me luck boys," he declared grinning lasciviously, and made his way over to the caravan which had now regained its equilibrium.

As they passed each other, Peter uttered just one word, "Wow!"

Jimmy knocked on the door. There was no reply. He knocked again, more loudly. "There's no bloody answer," he complained. He tried the door. It opened and he called out, "Hello, are you free?" and ventured inside. Ten seconds later he re-appeared at the door and mumbled, "There's nobody in there." That was just before he noticed the six grown men – his so-called friends and their new mate, Peter, 'The Rocker' – doubled up and roaring with laughter just across the yard.

"You Bastards! You Absolute Bastards!"

How everyone had kept a straight-face throughout the deception would be a topic of conversation for several weeks afterwards.

***

When All is Said and Done

During the so-called pandemic he had become jaded. So downhearted with the unrelenting pessimism and negativity which assaulted his senses day after day, that he'd seriously considered throwing himself from his bedroom window. Then he remembered that he lived in a ground floor flat.

Ultimately, this turned out to be a good thing. Had he lived in a high-rise tower block, this book may never have been written ...

***

Acknowledgements

Thanks to all the friends who generously gave their time to read the many versions of my scripts, gently pointing out any errors and suggesting occasional modifications and amendments, several of which were helpfully thought-provoking. None more so than my cousin Stuart Heaver who has probably enjoyed the chance to get his own back after I proofread and critiqued his exceptional book, *The Coal Black Sea*, a compelling and touching read which I can heartily recommend. Working with Stuart provided the catalyst for me to start writing this book.

And finally a special thank you goes to my beloved friend and constant source of inspiration, Sara Zúñiga, whose ardent support encouraged me to share my stories and motivated me to achieve my writing ambitions.

About the author

After retiring from full-time employment in November 2019 and having had his plans to tour the UK on his motorcycle thwarted by the Covid pandemic in 2020, Dave decided to use the 'era of lockdown' to finally realise a long-held ambition and take up a new venture as a writer.

This initially focussed on a memoir, *Mustn't Grumble*, and whilst working on that, he also decided to assemble a collection of some of the short stories which he had written over a period of almost twenty years.

This anthology, *One Day in a Lifetime* is the conclusion of that decision.

***

9 781787 920019